"I'm getting eaten alive. I'd better go," Sue Ellen said.

"Steer clear of the perfume."

"Don't worry! I never make the same mistake twice. Except for my choice of husbands, that is."

She started for her tent, turned back.

"Thanks, Joe. I understand a little better where you're coming from and where you want to go with this program. I also understand why you wanted me to see the operation firsthand."

Not hardly, thought Joe as he watched her cross the clearing. Joe had been all too aware of the woman beneath the power suit since their first confrontation.

Joe's suggestion to his Washington pal that the Department of Labor's northwest Florida regional director should personally evaluate his program had been legit. Not so legit was the mental image he'd formed of Ms. Carson minus the power suit and stripped down to the bare essentials.

Not many top-level government execs came packaged with a set of curves that spelled danger to any male past puberty.

Merline Lovelace

After twenty-three years in the United States Air Force,
pulling tours in Vietnam, at the Pentagon and at bases all
over the world, Merline Lovelace decided to try her hand
at writing. She now has more than sixty published novels
and over eight million copies of her works in print.

Merline and her own handsome hero live in Oklahoma.
When she's not glued to her keyboard, she loves traveling
to exotic locations, chasing little white balls around the
golf course and long, lazy dinners with family and friends.

Be sure to watch for Merline's next book, *Match Play*,
coming from Silhouette Romantic Suspense in
February 2008.

MERLINE
LOVELACE

RISKY BUSINESS

RISKY BUSINESS

copyright © 2008 by Merline Lovelace

isbn-13:978-0-373-88149-9

isbn-10:   0-373-88149-5

TheNextNovel.com

 HARLEQUIN®

PRINTED IN U.S.A.

From the Author

Dear Reader,

Have you ever had that perfect summer? I had several as a kid, but the summer I went off to camp wasn't one of them. That's when I discovered I'd *much* rather read Nancy Drew by flashlight than tell scary stories and swat mosquitoes at a marshmallow roast. Matters didn't improve much with adulthood, when up-close-and-personal encounters with snakes, wood ticks and poison oak convinced me I just wasn't cut out to be a nature girl.

So this book is for all of us who've tried—really tried—to appreciate the great outdoors. Hope you enjoy it!

All my best,

Merline

To the real Susie who, like the heroine of this book, left an indelible mark in the field of employment and training—and who introduced me to the wonderful world of romance novels that hot, long-ago summer in San Antonio.

Sue Ellen Carson was on a roll.

She loved her job as chief of the Department of Labor's Employment and Training Administration office in Pensacola, Florida. Her lawyer had finally convinced a judge to kill the alimony she'd had to pay the jerk she'd married on the rebound. Just last year she'd talked her very best friend into moving to the Florida Panhandle, then got to watch Andi and *her* former husband strike red-hot sparks off each other before tumbling back into love.

And, as frosting on the cake, Sue Ellen had a studly young Adonis in her bed on a semiregular basis.

Life was good. Very good.

Until her intercom buzzed that fateful Friday afternoon.

Informed that her Atlanta-based boss was on the line, Sue Ellen punched the speaker button and kicked back in her executive desk chair.

"Hey, Evan," she said in her soft, peaches-and-cream

drawl. She'd left her native Georgia decades ago, but the South never left the girl. "What's up?"

"My blood pressure, for one thing. I just got off the phone with Washington."

"Uh-oh. Congress isn't trying to cut the Job Corps budget again, are they?"

"They're always trying to cut the Job Corps budget."

Evan Greenberg was a good man and a good boss, who believed passionately in the Employment and Training Administration's charter of stimulating the U.S. labor market by providing high-quality job training, employment and information to employers and potential employees alike. Since ETA accomplished its mission primarily through state and local agencies, he arm-wrestled regularly with everyone from governors to owners of mom-and-pop, street-corner shops.

He was also a man of few words. As gruff as ever, Evan cut right to the purpose of his call. "Pack your bug spray, Sue Ellen. You're going to camp."

"Pardon me?"

"Three weeks of survival training. You start on Monday."

Her first thought was that he'd taken his concern for the health and physical fitness of ETA employees to new and ridiculous lengths. Her second, that he was getting back at her for the singing undertaker and bouquet of black balloons she'd sent for his fiftieth birthday.

"This is a joke, right?"

"Wrong. I told you, I just got off the phone with Washington. The order came right from the top."

"*What* order?"

"You. Camp. To evaluate Phase One of the disadvantaged-youth training program proposed by that Air Force guy in your region. What's his name?"

Understanding burst inside Sue Ellen's head like a Roman candle. Her jaws locked, then cracked just enough for her to grind out the name of the culprit.

"Chief Master Sergeant Joe Goodwin."

"Yeah, that's him. Evidently Goodwin has friends in high places. The director said she got the word directly from the White House. Since you're the one who nixed federal funding for his program, the powers-that-be think you should take another look at it, do an in-depth, hands-on review this time. That translates to three weeks at boot camp."

Digging in the spike heels she wore to add height to her petite, five-two frame, Sue Ellen pushed out of her chair. Her slim black skirt restricted her furious stride, but she couldn't take this sitting down.

Damn Goodwin! Where did he get off, going behind her back like this? Or pulling such powerful strings?

"I've got a slew of meetings scheduled over the next few

weeks," she protested. "And a two-day apprenticeship conference to attend."

Not to mention the cocktail party her friend Andi was throwing for seventy-five local bigwigs. Recently elected mayor of the small town of Gulf Springs, Andi was making a splash in regional politics. Sue Ellen had already decided Andi's next stop was the Florida State House, then the governor's office.

"I can't just drop everything to roast rattlesnake over a campfire," she protested.

Even as she voiced them, she knew her objections were futile. As a career civil servant, she worked for the director of the Employment and Training Administration, who worked for the secretary of labor, who worked for the president.

She was going to camp.

Her boss understood the chain of command as well as she did. Refusing to argue or debate the matter, Evan merely instructed her to clear her schedule.

"Don't forget the bug spray," he added on a parting note. "You're going to need it."

Sue Ellen bit back the retort that sprang to her lips. She was too professional to let rip.

The professionalism hadn't come easy. She'd worked damned hard to get where she was. Joining the civil service as a lowly GS-2, she'd had to take whatever job she could get every time her first husband was transferred. After their divorce, she'd focused on her own career, landed a job with the Department of Labor and soon shot up through the ranks.

Over the years, success and increasing responsibilities had added a patina of sophistication to the down-home, country girl from Valdosta, Georgia. Moving in ever higher circles had also introduced her to the handsome, smooth-talking con artist who'd charmed her into a second marriage. Luckily, she'd dumped the bastard before his shady deals could damage her reputation or her career.

Now an executive with a multimillion-dollar operating budget and more than fifty employees under her direct supervision, Sue Ellen rarely, if ever, resorted to expletives. She had to swallow several particularly ripe ones, however, before stabbing the intercom button again and instructing her assistant to get Chief Master Sergeant Joe Goodwin on the line.

Alicia came back a few moments later with word that the chief was unavailable. "They said he's wearing a halo. I didn't quite understand the reference."

Sue Ellen's first husband had been Air Force. She interpreted for her assistant. "I suspect they meant he's *doing* a HALO. That's a high-altitude, low-opening parachute jump."

"Oh. Well, they also said Goodwin left a message in case you tried to reach him. He can swing by your office around five, if you'll still be here."

"Call them back." There was nothing soft or peachy in her clipped instruction. "Have them tell the chief I'll be waiting at five sharp, armed and ready."

"Huh?"

"He'll get the drift. In the meantime, we need to cancel all my appointments and clear my calendar for the next three weeks."

Alicia let out a small screech. "Are you serious?"

"Unfortunately."

"You really want to cancel the meeting with the Okaloosa and Escambia county mayors? It took me weeks to find a time when everyone could get together."

"Sorry, but you'll have to reschedule. And please bring me the application for federal funding on the program Chief Goodwin proposed."

Her shell-shocked assistant carried in the thick file a few moments later. Sue Ellen set her jaw and opened the file.

Yep, there it was. Right on top. Her letter denying federal funds to supplement state and local contributions for a four-phase summer program Goodwin had labeled STEP.

What was it with the military? Did everything have to have its own acronym? Fuming, she flipped to the next page.

From previous reading, Sue Ellen knew this particular acronym stood for Survival, Team-building, Employment and a community-based Project. The summer-long program targeted at-risk kids between the ages of sixteen and eighteen. Old enough to work, but still young enough to be classified as juveniles by the legal system most of them had tripped over.

She didn't object to the team-building phase. Game-based, it was designed to teach the kind of leader-and-follower skills required to succeed in a work environment. Nor did she have a problem with the employment phase. Goodwin had lined up a number of local employers willing to give the participants in his program a summer job, which dovetailed nicely with some of ETA's own first-step initiatives.

And his final phase had actually won her admiration. It required the participants to collaborate on a public-works type project, thus encouraging them to give back to the community and fostering a sense of belonging among kids who'd been rejected too many times.

It was Phase One that had forced Sue Ellen to disapprove federal funding for the program. She agreed learning to survive in the wilderness was probably a good thing. For some people. But rubbing two sticks together to start a campfire didn't translate into usable workplace skills for anyone except maybe forest rangers and potential arsonists.

Then there was the fact that Goodwin proposed using off-duty, volunteer instructors from nearby Hurlburt Field, home of the air force's Special Operations Command, to conduct Phase One. Sue Ellen didn't go so far as to suspect these instructors would try to recruit the teens in their charge. On the other hand, with the war in Iraq becoming increasingly unpopular, she'd heard the army was offering twenty-thousand-dollar enlistment bonuses to recruits with certain skills. What better way to home-grow those skills than at a summer "survival" camp?

Lips pursed, she flipped through her letters suggesting the chief delete Phase One, along with his replies flatly refusing to do so. The file also contained memos for record of the meeting they'd had to try and find a middle ground. That meeting had taken place more than six months ago. When Sue Ellen hadn't heard back from him, she figured he'd shelved the concept.

Obviously, she'd figured wrong. Although why he'd waited so long to execute this end run was a mystery—one she intended to solve come five o'clock.

SHE WAS GIRDED FOR BATTLE when Goodwin arrived later that afternoon.

She'd met the man on several previous occasions, once

at her friend Andi's bookstore and once to try to resolve the issue of Phase One. At Andi's store he'd been in jeans and a T-shirt that stretched tight across rippling pecs and laser-incised lats. On the second occasion, he'd dressed for their meetings in the standard Florida business attire of slacks and an open-necked short-sleeved shirt.

When Goodwin strode into her office at precisely 5:01, he was still in his military uniform. His maroon beret sat low on his forehead. His sand-hued desert BDUs bristled with subdued insignias and patches that Sue Ellen guessed meant he could infiltrate any remote patch on the globe by air, sea or camel. The rack of stripes on each sleeve spoke for themselves. She knew no one achieved the rank of chief master sergeant in the elite Special Ops community unless they were tougher than kryptonite and meaner than barbed wire.

He wasn't the only one in the room with a steel backbone, however. Despite her scant inches, pansy-purple eyes and preference for ankle bracelets and strappy sandals over lace-up combat boots, Sue Ellen hadn't reached *her* position by rolling over and playing dead when confronted with very large, very intimidating males. Lifting her chin, she issued a cool greeting.

"Chief."

"Ms. Carson."

He dragged off his beret and stuffed it in the leg pocket of his BDUs. Removing that symbol of lethal power didn't do much to soften his image. Skin tanned to leather and salt-and-pepper hair shaved so close to the scalp as to make him appear almost bald still sent distinct, don't-mess-with-me signals.

"Have a seat."

She waved him to one of the chairs in front of her desk, in no mood to offer more casual seating at the round conference table in the corner of her office. Nor did she intend to give him the edge by admitting she'd been railroaded into attending his damned camp. Let him drag it out of her.

"I understand we need to talk about STEP," she said, still cool, still polite.

"We do. Before we get started, you might want to take a look at these."

He delved into the pocket on his other pant leg and produced a folded manila envelope. From that he extracted several documents.

"This gives the name and background information on the teen you'll be paired with during survival training. I've also brought a brochure detailing what to bring with you."

So much for digging it out of her! He must have received a call notifying him about her participation around the same time Sue Ellen's boss had contacted her.

He nudged the folded papers across her desk. She didn't so much as glance at them.

"I don't appreciate this end run, Chief. How would you like it if one of your men jumped the chain of command and went straight to the top?"

"None of my men would jump the chain of command."

The flat arrogance of that came close to unleashing Sue Ellen's simmering temper. She held it in by a sheer effort of will.

"Forcing my hand is hardly the way to win my support or approval," she said icily.

"I know. I'm sorry 'bout that."

He had the grace to look contrite for a second or two, but ruined the effect by rolling those wide shoulders in a shrug.

"Guess I'd better clear the air, or try to. I never intended to go around you. The truth is, I'd given up on securing federal funding for the STEP program. I've been pressing ahead using state and local support."

"So why the abrupt change in direction?"

"I made a quick trip to a classified location a few weeks back. I can't go into details, but the, ah, individual my team extracted has friends in…"

"Let me guess," Sue Ellen drawled. "In high places."

A smile tugged at his lips. Looking anything but apologetic now, he nodded. "Very high places."

"So you asked this friend to intervene? And you don't call that jumping the chain of command?"

"Actually, one of my men let drop that the mission was my last. When the, uh, individual asked what I planned to do after I hung up my uniform, I told him about the STEP program." The smile made it to his gold-flecked brown eyes. "I may have mentioned in passing the problem with ETA."

"Right," Sue Ellen huffed. "In passing."

She supposed she couldn't really hold the back-door influence against him. Goodwin had put months of research and effort into developing his program. In his position, she would have pulled every available string, too.

"When do you separate from the air force?"

"Today's my last day on active duty." The smile didn't waver, but there was no mistaking the regret in his deep voice. "I start terminal leave tomorrow and officially retire at the end of the month."

"This is what you're going to do full-time when you retire? Teach survival skills to disadvantaged kids?"

"It's what I hope to do full-time. Depends on how the trial program goes. Which brings me back to the teen you'll be paired with."

He indicated the folded envelope with a jerk of his chin.

"Her name is Rose Gutierrez. I had a sponsor lined up for her, but the woman had to drop out at the last minute."

Smart move, Sue Ellen thought cynically.

"Rose has had a rough time," the chief continued. "STEP is her last stop before a juvenile detention center."

Sue Ellen didn't like the sound of that. Frowning, she glanced at the papers with a frisson of alarm. Who had Goodwin paired her with? And what exactly did "pairing" entail, anyway? Before she could ask, his gaze locked with hers. All trace of a smile had disappeared from his eyes.

"That's why I wanted to see you this afternoon."

"To warn me about Rose?"

"To let you take out your anger at being coerced on me, so you don't take it out on her."

Sue Ellen sucked in a swift breath. Not only had the man gone over her head, he had the unmitigated gall to sit there and suggest she would actually put their private differences ahead of an adolescent's welfare.

"I was angry before," she said, her eyes narrowed to slits. "Now I'm *pissed*."

Joe felt the impact of that dagger glare right down to his boot tops. He'd racked up twenty-six years in uniform, most of them in Special Ops. During those years he'd honed his instincts to a razor's edge—and every one of them was now shouting that he'd just made a serious tactical error.

Until this point he'd held two competing but not necessarily contradictory opinions of Ms. Sue Ellen Carson. First, she was all woman. Her feathery blond hair, heart-shaped face and deep purple eyes came packaged with a seductive set of curves that could make a man trip over his own tongue. Second, she was a bureaucratic, bullheaded pain in the ass.

Viewing her now, with those amethyst eyes flashing and fury staining her cheeks, Joe amended his opinion to include a third view. The stubborn, delectable Ms. Carson was no lightweight. She looked ready to bite into him, chew him up and spit him out right then and there.

Joe didn't get that kind of ferocity from many men, let alone a slip of a female who wouldn't come up to his chin without the ankle-busting spike heels she was wearing. Thinking of her footwear reminded him of the second reason he'd driven all the way over to Pensacola for this face-to-face.

"I'll do my best to get you un-pissed in the next three weeks," he promised. "But first, you'd better make a quick trip to a camping or outdoor-recreation supply shop. Buy and bring only what's on the list. Save your receipts, as the program covers all associated expenses."

She unfroze enough to ask stiffly, "What are we talking here? Pup tents and bedrolls?"

"No, I strong-armed local merchants into providing the heavy stuff, as well as most of our sporting and navigational equipment. All you're encouraged to bring… Correction, all you're allowed to bring are the personal items on that list and any prescribed medications. Oh, and a good supply of bug spray."

With what sounded like a strangled groan, she reached for the envelope and slid out the camp brochure. Joe figured he'd better make his getaway before she skimmed the extremely abbreviated list of approved personal items. He had a feeling the elegant Ms. Carson was *not* going to be thrilled about having to wash her undies in swamp water every night.

"Call me if you have any questions." Tugging his beret from his leg pocket, he rose. "I included my home and cell phone numbers in the packet."

He almost made it to the door. A sharp exclamation brought him around.

"Goodwin!"

"Yeah?"

"I don't go anywhere without a cell phone." She rose to her feet and planted her hands on her desk. Both her voice and expression telegraphed a flat refusal to compromise. "It's a matter of safety, not convenience."

They'd reached their first critical make-or-break point and they hadn't even taken to the field yet. Joe knew he had to win this one or forget trying to convince her of the value of his program.

"That's the whole point of Phase One," he said evenly. "Teaching participants to rely on themselves, not mechanical devices that could fail or might not be available in a crisis situation."

"This is a deal-breaker, Goodwin. I have responsibilities. Not to mention a life. I need to be able to contact the outside world, and have them contact me in an emergency."

"Base camp will have phones for emergency contact. The instructors will carry radios. I guarantee you'll be notified of any emergencies." He palmed the thin fuzz covering his scalp. "Try it for the first week my way. If that doesn't work, we'll reassess the situation. Deal?"

He thought for a moment she was going to refuse. Her mouth opened. Shut with a snap. Finally, she dipped her head in a curt nod.

"Deal."

CHAPTER 2

"I still can't believe I'm doing this."

Glumly, Sue Ellen used a toothpick to push an olive around her martini glass. Her friend Andi had invited her over for a lazy Sunday evening dinner—the condemned's last meal before departing for survival training at 6:00 a.m. the following morning.

"Three weeks with no alcohol," Sue Ellen muttered, stabbing at the olive, "no makeup and no sex."

Her glance drifted to the French doors leading to the deck. Andi's husband, Dave, was out there doing his man-thing with the grill. Sue Ellen's handsome young stud stood next to him, beer in hand.

Major Bill Steadman had been part of her life for almost a year now, off and on. They enjoyed each other's company. They enjoyed even more the no-holds-barred sex. That was enough for both of them.

Bill, known by the nickname Crash among friends and fellow officers, was still very quietly and very privately hurting over the death of his wife some years ago. For Sue Ellen, two husbands constituted one too many. The first one had damned near broken her heart when he'd decided he was tired of being married. The second had emptied her savings account before she booted the smooth-talking sleaze out of her life.

As painful as they were at the time, Sue Ellen's two divorces had molded her into the woman she now was. Independent. Self-reliant. Able to enjoy the companionship of handsome males without experiencing the pesky urge to nest. She considered her life perfect just the way it was—and would be again, once she got through the next three weeks.

Propping her elbows on the massive slab of marble that served as Andi's kitchen counter, she crossed one smooth-shaven leg over the other. "Tell me about Joe Goodwin," she said to the tall, vibrant brunette she'd shared so many secrets and spa sessions with. "What's his Achilles heel?"

Andi looked up from slicing a loaf of crusty Italian bread, her green eyes alight with laughter. "He doesn't have an Achilles heel. He's Special Tactics."

Andi's husband had hung up his uniform last year after a career in the highly elite cadre known as Special Tactics. Dave Armstrong always maintained they were a breed apart, impervious to heat, cold and speeding bullets.

Sue Ellen wasn't buying it.

"Com'on, honey chile. You married, divorced and remarried one of those crazies. You know how their mind works. You also know this guy, Goodwin. Or Dave does. What pushes the man's buttons?"

"Sorry, S.E." Andi resumed her methodical slicing. "I can't help you there. I don't know much about Joe's personal life. I'm sure Dave does, but I've never asked him for details. He *has* told me the chief's men would follow him into hell and back. That's the highest praise Dave can give any man."

"Mmmm."

The noncommittal response brought Andi's knife to a standstill again. "From what you've told me, Sue Ellen, Phase One of the chief's STEP program is designed to teach at-risk kids to trust their instincts alone and as part of a team. I can't think of anyone more qualified to do that than Joe Goodwin," she finished as the door to the deck slid open.

"Do what?" her husband asked as he carried a platter heaped with the results of his grill endeavors into the kitchen. Crash followed with his beer and Dave's.

"Sue Ellen and I have been discussing her wilderness adventure. She still has doubts about it…and about Joe Goodwin's insistence that the participants will be able to translate what they learn into workplace skills."

"Joe knows whereof he speaks." Sliding the platter of sizzling steaks onto the counter, Dave gave Goodwin his highest endorsement. "Don't forget, he's…"

"We know, we know."

A laughing Andi raised both hands. Forefingers extended, she conducted an invisible orchestra.

"On the down beat. One, two…"

She and Sue Ellen sang out in chorus. "He's Special Tactics."

"Damn straight."

Grinning, Crash joined the trio at the counter and passed Dave his beer. "If those kids learn a fraction of what I did during survival, evasion and escape training, they'll bring some very unique skills to the workplace."

He curled a casual hand over Sue Ellen's nape and kneaded the warm skin. His palm was cool and damp from the beer, his fingers sure and strong. Delicious tingles rippled along Sue Ellen's spine.

The two men shared amused glances but let the subject drop. Crash didn't pick it up again until he'd driven Sue Ellen back to her bayside condo halfway between Pensacola and Andi's house in Gulf Springs.

A cool breeze off the bay ruffled the ends of her short blond shag as Crash walked her to her door. They'd already agreed he wouldn't come in. He had a flight to prebrief the next morning and Sue Ellen had to be up before dawn. The mere thought made her groan.

They settled for hot and hungry kisses at the front door. Crash propped one hand against her doorjamb while he took her mouth. His other hand played musical scales on her spine.

"You are *so* good with those fingers," she murmured against his mouth. "Is that one of the skills you picked up at survival school?"

"I did learn some handy massage techniques," he assured her with a grin. "Mostly involving smelly, grungy feet."

Sue Ellen couldn't help herself. He was so damned sexy with his short, curly hair and bedroom eyes. Hooking a sandaled foot around his calf, she rubbed it sensuously.

"Tell you what, sweet cheeks. When I get home, I'll practice whatever techniques *I* pick up on you."

His brows waggled in an exaggerated leer. "Starting with my feet?"

"I'll miss you," he said, swooping in for a last taste.

God, he was good! Sue Ellen had kissed—and been kissed—by her share of men. Some had turned her off, some had flicked the switch straight to on. Crash most definitely fell in the switch-flicking category. He did this delicious thing with his tongue, running it behind her teeth before playing touch tag with hers.

"I'll miss you, too," she murmured against his mouth. "See you in three weeks."

Sue Ellen paused with her hand on the front door latch, watching his easy stride as he headed for his car, wishing she'd insisted he come in, wondering why she hadn't.

She liked Crash. *Really* liked him. He was twelve years her junior, but he hadn't reached the rank of major and been selected as an instructor pilot by acting impulsive or immature. Never once in their relationship had Sue Ellen felt like the brassy older woman parading her handsome boy-toy around on a leash. Just the opposite, in fact. Crash took a very male, very smug delight in the envious glances aimed his way when he showed *her* off at squadron parties.

There was more to Bill Steadman than his cocky grin and pilot's swagger, however. He never talked about his wife's tragic death in a boating accident, but Sue Ellen knew he would always carry her in a corner of his heart. She suspected that was why he valued their straightforward, undemanding relationship as much as she did. He enjoyed the companionship, reveled in the sex and wasn't looking for anything more.

So why was she suddenly feeling so…so antsy?

Frowning, she locked the door behind her. It had to be this damned survival training. Traipsing into the boonies on short notice for three entire weeks had messed up her well-ordered schedule and thrown her off stride. Aside from the fact that she had serious reservations about the program, Sue Ellen wasn't the outdoorsy type. She flat hated the thought of trading her air-conditioned office and elegant condo for a pup tent.

Kicking off her platform sandals, she padded through the foyer of the condo she'd purchased after shedding husband number two. The two-bedroom, bayside unit was her haven as well as her home. She'd lovingly furnished it with an eclectic blend of colors and styles that reflected her personality.

The Italian marble tiles of the foyer were cool and smooth under her feet. She'd painted the long wall in the entryway a dramatic terra-cotta to showcase her collection of sea-shells. She'd started gathering them years ago, after finding a spiny pink murex more than a foot long during a walk along the beach. Since then she'd added a gleaming triton, a monster lion's paw and a pearly trochus, all individually illuminated by high-intensity spots and displayed on shelves Sue Ellen had finished with an antique gold crackle.

Vibrant earth tones and antiques filled the rest of the condo. She'd left three of the great room walls a creamy white. The fourth picked up the terra-cotta of the entryway and provided the perfect backdrop for the rolled-arm sofa and love seat she'd had recovered in a striped damask of shimmering green, gold and rust. A mirrored Louis XV armoire housed a bar and a fifty-CD player. The area rug had cost more than the rest of the room's pieces combined. Sue Ellen didn't care. Every time she sank her toes into the luxurious, tightly woven Karastan, she considered the money well spent.

The silky fibers provided their familiar sensual thrill as she padded across the great room to check the answering machine in the small alcove she'd converted to a home office. Tall, fluted white columns flanked the alcove, which held the lavishly trimmed rococo desk she'd picked up at an estate sale. The six-foot rubber plant that drooped gracefully next to the desk was one of her few leftovers from her days as an air force wife. Despite her first husband's repeated objections and the reluctance of movers to load the plant into their vans, it had made almost as many moves as Sue Ellen had.

"Hello, Ralph." She tested the glossy leaves in passing. "How's it hanging, pal?"

Judicious watering and regularly aerated soil had left Ralph hanging pretty well. Balancing on one foot, Sue Ellen rubbed the back of her calf with the other as she listened to several voice mails and noted phone numbers for return calls. That done, she slid the list of emergency contact numbers Chief Goodwin had included with his instruction packet toward her and hit the record button.

"Hey, y'all. I'm going incommunicado for a while. If you have a real emergency and need to get hold of me, call my office or one of these numbers."

She gave the numbers listed in the camp brochure, repeated them slowly and clicked off. Her next task was to boot up her laptop, check her e-mail and compose an automatic, out-of-office reply.

Her finger hovered over the save button for several seconds. The idea of no voice mail, text messaging or e-mail for three whole weeks made her nervous. She couldn't remember the last time she'd taken a vacation lasting more than eight or ten days. Even during that gloriously pampered week at a southern California spa, she'd stayed in contact with her office by cell phone.

Resentment flared anew at her imposed sentence. She took her job seriously, dammit. Had worked her tail off to make it to the executive ranks. Now some crusty chief master sergeant with a bug up his butt was hobbling her ability to respond to the inevitable crises that came with managerial responsibilities.

In the most literal sense of the cliché, Sue Ellen was *not* a happy camper. Her mouth set into tight lines, she went into the bedroom to stuff the meager assortment of allowed items into her new, sugar-pink knapsack.

Her last act before crawling into bed was to remove the

diamond stud in her belly button. She'd had her tummy pierced last year, figuring that was as good a use as any for the flashy engagement rock her second husband had purchased—using Sue Ellen's funds, she discovered later. She didn't harbor any particular fondness for the stone but couldn't see losing it during a swamp crossing or something equally unpleasant.

BEING REQUIRED TO REPORT to the assembly area before dawn the next morning didn't particularly improve Sue Ellen's mood.

She was waiting when Andi's cherry-red Tahoe pulled up at oh-dark-thirty. Lugging her knapsack, Sue Ellen set the alarm, locked the front door and climbed into the passenger seat. A life-restoring ambrosia scent wafted from the cardboard cups in twin holders.

"Is that coffee?"

"It is. I figured you'd need a jolt to get going."

"You figured right." Snagging one of the cups, Sue Ellen downed several life-restoring gulps. "Thanks for playing taxi driver for me."

"No problem." Grinning, Andi put the Tahoe in gear. "It was worth getting out of bed an hour early to see you in socks, hiking boots and cargo shorts. Did you pack plenty of bug spray?"

"Two cans and a tube of something guaranteed to repel everything from crocs to rabid dogs. With any luck," Sue Ellen muttered, "I'll stink so bad I'll get kicked out of camp my first day."

"I doubt your stench will deter Joe Goodwin." Andi dropped her voice an octave and grunted. "Remember, S.E., he's…"

"Special Tactics."

Their chorus didn't seem nearly as funny this morning as it had last night.

"Do I need to swing by and water Ralph the Rubber Tree?" Andi asked as she wheeled through the soft Florida dawn.

"I put him on a timer."

"How about your mail?"

"The post office is holding it."

"You don't need me to pay any bills?"

"They're all paid electronically." Grumbling, Sue Ellen buried her nose in her coffee mug. "All these arrangements, you'd think I was heading off for an around-the-world cruise. Which I might just do after this ordeal."

"Yeah, right. Like you're going to stay away from your office for another month or six weeks."

"It could happen."

Andi's mink-brown ponytail danced as she swung her

head in her passenger's direction. "Tell you what. You sign up for a cruise lasting more than five days and I'll sign Dave and me up, too."

"Honey chile," Sue Ellen drawled, "it would almost be worth missing another month of work to see mucho macho Dave Armstrong strolling a deck in flip-flops and sipping frou-frou drinks with little umbrellas."

"It could happen," her friend echoed with something less than complete conviction.

The two women whiled away the rest of the short drive entertaining themselves with fantasies about tropical islands and muscle-bound hunks slathered with sunscreen.

"God, I'd love to see Dave in a Speedo," Andi commented as she drove through the gathering dawn.

"Bet he'd look almost as good as Crash." A vision of her lover's sleek, muscled body floated across Sue Ellen's mental video screen. "'Course, Crash looks good in anything. Or *out* of it," she added with a smirk.

Andi shot her a curious glance. "You two have been seeing a lot of each other lately. You getting serious?"

"Nope. We like things just the way they are. Easy and uncomplicated."

Despite Sue Ellen's breezy reply, the question revived the doubts that had swirled around inside her head last night. Why hadn't she and Crash taken things to the next level?

She'd have to think about that in the next few weeks, she decided as they wheeled into the McDonald's parking lot Chief Goodwin had designated as the rendezvous point.

A small crowd had already gathered. Mom, dads or guardians were saying farewell to an assortment of men, women and teens, none of whom looked particularly thrilled to have been rousted out of bed before dawn. The sight of a uniformed police officer standing beside the open door of a patrol car didn't do a whole lot for Sue Ellen's enthusiasm, either.

Andi put the Tahoe in Park and ambled beside Sue Ellen as she hauled her knapsack over to the group. Goodwin stood in the middle of things, clipboard in hand. He was wearing baggy woodland camouflage pants, a black T-shirt with STEP stenciled in white letters across the back and a floppy-brimmed boonie hat. When the two women approached, he pushed the hat back and greeted Andi with a grin.

"'Morning, Madam Mayor."

Andi made a face, still not quite used to the title she'd acquired in the last election. "'Morning, Chief. I brought your reluctant recruit."

"So I see." His glance went to Sue Ellen and checked her over from ball cap to bootlaces. "You find everything on the checklist okay?"

"Sure did." She hefted the knapsack. "I have all ten essentials."

Plus a few items that weren't on the list. They weighted her knapsack a bit, but Sue Ellen figured she could always jettison the paperback novel and sugared pecans if absolutely necessary. The aloe wet wipes would be the last item to go, though.

"Any cell phones?" Goodwin asked with a hook of one brow.

"No."

"Good." Approval gleamed in his whiskey-brown eyes. "You probably wouldn't get a signal out where we're heading, anyway."

"That did occur to me."

"We'll load up in a few minutes. You ready to meet your tent mate?"

As ready as she'd ever be. The brief background sketch Goodwin had provided only increased Sue Ellen's doubts about this whole venture. Feeling as skittish as a kid going off to school the first day, she gave Andi a quick hug.

"Thanks for the ride."

"You're welcome." She returned the hug and issued a stern order to Goodwin. "Make sure you bring her back in one piece."

"I'll do my best."

On that somewhat less-than-reassuring note, Goodwin escorted Sue Ellen through the muddle of knapsacks and milling campers. Most of the boys were still in the long-haired, acne stage. By contrast, the sixteen- and seventeen-year-old girls filled out their tank tops and jeans with jailbait curves.

Sue Ellen glanced hopefully at a chubby, cheerful blond with a mouth full of metal and colored rubber bands. To her disappointment, Goodwin led her right past that girl to one standing with her shoulders propped against the side of the bus. Arms folded, mouth sulky, she looked as unhappy to be there as Sue Ellen was.

Like the other girls, she showed ripe curves under her jeans and tank top. Her shaggy, shoulder-length black hair needed a good cut to lighten the heavy layers, Sue Ellen thought, and she wore a little too much eye makeup, but she had the makings of a beauty under that sullen, resentful mask.

"Rose, this is your partner, Sue Ellen Carson."

The dark eyes shifted. The resentment didn't.

Pasting on a smile, Sue Ellen held out her hand. "Hi, Rose. Sorry you got stuck with me at the last minute."

The teen's arms remained tightly folded. After an awkward pause, Sue Ellen dropped her hand.

"You'll have time to get to know each other on the

drive out to the camp," Goodwin said, unperturbed by the girl's rudeness. "Better hit the bathroom before we go. It's a long ride."

Rose straightened and stalked off without a word. As Sue Ellen lugged her backpack to the bus, one thought looped repeatedly through her mind.

Oh, this was going to be fun.

CHAPTER 3

The bus ride to the campsite took upward of an hour and a half.

Ten minutes out, Sue Ellen drained the dregs of her coffee and crunched the cardboard cup. Tucking it in a pocket of her backpack, she did as the chief had suggested and tried to use the time to get to know the girl sitting next to her.

Despite her best efforts, all she could pry out of Rose were monosyllabic replies—when she could get a response at all. The teen kept her arms hitched tight around her backpack, her face turned to the window and her gaze on the tall, spindly pines rolling by.

When tastes in music and favorite books bombed as conversational gambits, Sue Ellen tried school. "I understand you go to George Marshall High."

No response.

"Did I read in the newspaper that the school's getting a new gymnasium?"

A shrug.

"So what's your favorite subject?"

Silence.

"Com'on, Rose, ya gotta give me something to work with here."

The girl's head slewed around. Disdain and dislike warred for supremacy in her dark eyes. "Why?"

Sue Ellen thought the reason would be obvious, even to an obnoxious sixteen-year-old, but heroically refrained from saying so.

"Because we're going to be sharing a tent for three weeks," she said, adding a conspiratorial wink. "Just between you and me, I'm not real happy about the tent bit. I'd much rather we camp out in a nice, air-conditioned room in a beachfront hotel."

Her blend of honesty and levity failed to produce so much as a dent.

"I could be wrong," Sue Ellen mused, "but I'm getting the impression you're not particularly thrilled about camping out, either."

"You got that right."

Eureka! Four whole words.

She was basking in the glow of victory when Rose cranked her face around and presented the back of her head again. Sue Ellen clamped her lips over a spurt of real annoyance.

Her irritation faded, however, when Rose's thick hair fell forward over her shoulder to reveal livid bruises on her neck. Good Lord! Those looked like finger imprints.

Dismayed by the ugly marks, Sue Ellen searched her mind for the scant facts Chief Goodwin had provided in Rose's profile. Left alone as a four-year-old when her crack-addicted mother went out to score a hit and subsequently OD'd. Father unknown. Placed in a series of foster homes. Twice picked up as a runaway. Arrested a few weeks ago for "borrowing" a neighbor's car without his knowledge or consent. Currently in the custody of a couple who cared for three other foster children in addition to three of their own.

Rose faced time in a juvenile detention center if she didn't successfully complete STEP, but neither of her foster parents had been able—willing?—to trek off into the wilderness for three whole weeks. Sue Ellen wouldn't exactly qualify as willing, either, but the bruises on Rose's neck knocked her resentment down a few pegs.

Had Goodwin seen those marks? Should she mention them if he hadn't? Chewing on the inside of her lip, Sue Ellen decided not to say anything yet. She wouldn't earn Rose's trust by running to the chief the first day. She'd draw the girl out, learn the circumstances, and then decide what to do about them.

Although she'd met with zero success so far, Sue Ellen

was confident she'd penetrate Rose's prickly barriers sooner or later. She'd attended dozens of on-the-job training courses covering everything from employee goal-setting to sexual harassment in the workplace. She'd also completed a master's degree in labor management. Surely she possessed the necessary interpersonal skills to communicate with a sixteen-year-old.

OR NOT, SHE THOUGHT an hour later.

Hot and seriously annoyed after a long ride spent chatting with everyone around her except Rose, Sue Ellen stood with the others in a clearing hacked out of the pines. That's all it was, a rough patch of sandy, scrub-covered dirt. A small stream meandered along one edge of the perimeter and provided the only running water. The large, mud-brown tent in the center, the campers were informed, would serve as combination mess tent, recreation center and dispensary. Sue Ellen sincerely hoped the ATVs parked beside the tent were for the campers to use and enjoy, but suspected they were for emergency transportation only.

"Okay, folks. Gather round."

His face shaded by the brim of his hat, Goodwin eyed the thirty participants in Phase One.

"The first order of business is to divide you into teams. Then you'll set up your bivouac areas."

Goodwin separated them into groups of ten and dubbed the teams the Reds Blues and Yellows. The instructors were the blacks. After passing out T-shirts in appropriate colors, he and his crew divvied up a small mountain of equipment and suggested the teams pick a corner of the clearing to set up their separate areas.

Sue Ellen was on the Blue team. Glancing at her fellow Blues, she had to admit they didn't inspire a great deal of confidence. Next to her stood a truck driver and his son, neither of whom appeared to be speaking to the other. Another teen was accompanied by his older brother, who administered a whap to the back of the head every time the kid let slip with a four-letter word. In the short time since they'd arrived, there'd been several whaps. A thin, twitchy librarian from the local community college stood next to the boy he'd agreed to sponsor. The blond girl with the bubbly smile and mouthful of braces was also a Blue, along with her mother.

Then there was Rose. The girl had swept a scornful glance over her teammates before dropping her backpack to the dirt and plunking down on it. She sat there now with a look of acute boredom on her face while the other nine Blues surveyed the pile of equipment they'd been allotted.

"Anyone know how to set up a pup tent?" Sue Ellen asked with a hopeful glance around the circle.

"I do, I do." Flashing a metallic smile, the chubby blond waved a hand. "I helped my brother set one up in the back yard, didn't I, Mom?"

Her tired-looking mother sagged at the shoulders. "No, Brenda, you didn't."

"Sure I did."

"Sweetie, you watched while he draped a blanket over the clothesline."

"So? That was helping."

"Com'on, Bren. You promised you wouldn't, uh, exaggerate while we're here, remember?"

"Okay, okay."

Sue Ellen thought the truck driver and his burly son might possess some camping skills, but the father shrugged and the scowling boy just stood with his hands shoved into the pockets of his cutoffs.

At that point the younger of the two brothers dragged one of the tent bags from the pile. "Ain't no big fu—"

A thump on the head from his sibling cut him off. Glaring, he started again.

"Ain't no big friggin' deal. All you gotta do is stick a pole in the ground."

Erecting the two-person tents turned out to involve more than mere pole sticking, but eventually five lopsided structures dotted the Blue corner of the field.

The librarian surveyed their accomplishments dubiously. "Now what?"

Sue Ellen waited for someone to make a suggestion. She didn't want to jump into the lead for their small group. After several silent beats, it was obvious someone had to.

"Since we don't seem to have anything else on the immediate agenda, why don't we get comfortable and learn a little about one another?"

Dragging her waterproof slicker out of her knapsack, she spread it on the sandy soil. The others followed suit, except for Rose, who disdained to be part of the group. Sue Ellen ignored her and smiled brightly at the other eight.

"Who wants to start?"

After several hesitant moments, the librarian introduced himself as Roger Bendix and the boy he'd agreed to sponsor as Dylan Thomas. Smiling, Roger nudged his glasses higher on his nose with a forefinger.

"How could I *not* volunteer to sponsor someone named after the greatest poet of the twentieth century?"

Dylan snorted and rolled his eyes. "My mom says she named me after the rock star. Said she dropped acid at one of his concerts and got laid, right there in the aisle. And she wonders why I smoke an occasional joint," he added with a disgusted shake of his head.

Ooooh-kay.

The truck driver gave his name as Paul D'Raggio. His son was Paul Jr., and a lazy, no-account loser, according to his loving father.

The brothers were Everett and Jackson McPhee. Ev played football at the University of Florida, but was missing summer practice and now risked being cut from the team because of his decision to see Jackson through STEP.

"Young punk's a half step away from jail." The beefy tackle delivered another thump to his sibling's head. "Took part in a gang brawl that ended in several torched vehicles."

"I didn't set fire to nothin'. The brothers done it."

"His street brothers," Ev clarified. "Damn fools, every one of 'em."

Cheerful, chubby Brenda went next and blithely informed the group she'd just been kicked out of high school for making up tales about her teachers' supposedly torrid affairs with students. Sighing, her mother introduced herself as Delilah Evans.

"I'm a full-time mom. I trained as a nurse but quit to raise my kids. I have three, although—" her mouth stretched into a determined smile "—my oldest seems to demand most of my attention."

Joe Goodwin was right, Sue Ellen thought on a ripple of dismay. All of these kids teetered right on the edge. Whether three weeks puttering around among the pines would keep them from toppling into the abyss remained to be seen, however.

"I'm Sue Ellen Carson," she said, since it was her turn. "I'm divorced, live with a plant named Ralph and work for the Department of Labor."

Nothing like stripping her life down to the bare essentials!

"I'm here with Rose Gutierrez. Who," she continued when her tent mate remained silent, "will tell us about herself when she feels more comfortable about opening up."

"What do we do now?" Roger asked after a moment, inching up his glasses again.

No one seemed to have any idea. They looked to the Black Shirts for guidance, but the instructors were hunkered down with their heads together over what looked like a detailed, terrain-contour map.

Sue Ellen didn't like the look of that map. The unfolded page seemed to cover a considerable amount of territory. She liked it even less when Goodwin folded the map, issued a few words to his instructors and rose.

"Okay, teams. Now that you're set up, we'll head out on a short hike to familiarize you with the area and terrain. Reds will go east. Yellows, you head west. Blues, northeast. Two Blacks will accompany each group. Whenever you're ready."

The teams waited for more guidance. Like, how long

was short? And which way was northeast? When none was forthcoming, the groups milled around for a while. Finally, Sue Ellen went back to her tent and began lightening her backpack.

"I'm not lugging all this stuff along with me."

Goodwin hooked a brow but made no comment as she dumped several items on his list of must-haves. Her extra set of underwear went into her pup tent alongside the flashlight. With the sun blazing down and the heat suffocating the air, she didn't figure she'd need the waterproof sheet or her jeans. The trail mix and dried fruit, either, although she might take a PowerBar for a midmorning snack. She debated over the spare bootlaces and decided they didn't weigh that much. One thing for sure, she wasn't going into the bush— or behind one—without a package of moist towelettes.

The others hesitated a few moments before following her lead. Their backpacks considerably lightened, they gathered in front of their tents.

"All set?" Goodwin asked.

"All set," Sue Ellen confirmed.

Nodding, he shouldered his own, much heavier pack. Another similarly laden Black shirt joined the group. Sue Ellen judged the lean, tough-looking Latino to be younger than the chief by a good fifteen years.

"For those of you who haven't met him," Goodwin said, "this is Rafael Smith."

A stir of movement at Sue Ellen's side snagged her gaze. Rose had squared her shoulders and was almost—almost!—cracking a smile. The upward curve to her lips took a dive the instant she noticed Sue Ellen's eyes on her.

Prepped and ready, the Blues waited for Goodwin or Smith to begin the march. Neither man moved. Finally, a nervous Roger noted that the Reds and Yellows had started out.

"What are we waiting for?" he asked hesitantly.

"For one of you to take the lead," Goodwin answered calmly.

"One of us?"

"That's right. Rafe and I will accompany you to point out hazards and share our knowledge when appropriate, but you folks set the pace and the direction. Just head in a generally northeast direction."

Roger pursed his lips and consulted his watch, which contained more buttons and dials than a 747 console. One of the dials must have been a compass, because he stepped out.

At what Sue Ellen assumed was the northeast corner of the clearing, they were presented with a choice of trails. One followed the left bank of the sandy-bottomed stream.

Another threaded through stands of tall, long-leaf pines
and red oak. The neatly folded map Roger consulted identified the second, barely discernible trail as an old logging
road.

The librarian looked to the chief once more and got no
help there. Lips pursed, he consulted his fellow Blues. "Any
preference?"

"Don't make us no nevermind," Ev said with a shrug of
his massive shoulders.

"Six of one, half dozen of the other," Paul Sr. agreed.

Brenda and her mom had no opinion, either. Rose, no
doubt prompted by the presence of Rafe, stirred herself
enough to mutter, "Whatever."

That forced Sue Ellen into leadership mode again.
Hiding her dismay at the group's collective indecision, she
proposed a suggestion.

"Why don't we head out following the stream and come
back via the road?"

Their choice made, the Blues fell into single file. Roger
and Dylan took the point, as Goodwin described it. The
chief fell in behind them, with Brenda and her mom trailing
him. Rafe dropped back to the rear. Rose dragged her feet
and did the same. Sue Ellen was bracketed between the
Pauls, Jr. and Sr., and the McPhee brothers.

Five minutes into their trek, the Blues were muttering and

ducking and sidestepping to avoid branches and prickly underbrush. Ten minutes later, those in the group wearing shorts were shooting nasty looks over their shoulders at Sue Ellen.

"Why'd you tell us to take our long pants out of our knapsacks?" Ev grumbled.

"I didn't tell you to do anything. I merely lightened my load. You all decided to do the same."

"Yeah, well, we thought you knew what you were doin'."

She'd thought the same. Ruefully, Sue Ellen realized the leadership skills she exercised daily in her job might not serve her as well here in the wilds. Her eyes on the low-hanging limb Ev held back for her, she missed the bushy palmetto below. Its sharply serrated leaf sliced into her calf like a razor. Glistening red welled up instantly from the cut.

"Dammit!"

Ev turned back, spotted the blood and cupped his hands around his mouth. "Hey! Chief! We got us a walking wounded here."

Goodwin wove his way back through the group. "What happened?"

"Damned plant jumped out and bit me," Sue Ellen grumbled.

"That's a saw palm. You want to steer around those."

"Now he tells us."

Ignoring her sarcastic drawl, Goodwin shrugged out of his backpack and hunkered down. A moment later he extracted a first aid kit. Sue Ellen scowled down at his bent head as he tore the wrapping from a gauze pad.

"You could have warned us we'd need long pants for this little hike."

"I could have," he agreed. "But then you wouldn't have learned the most basic rule of survival."

"Don't get bit by man-eating plants?"

"Don't go into the field without planning for a worst-case scenario."

Grasping her leg just above the boot, he rested it on his bent knee. His palm was warm and rough against Sue Ellen's skin, his touch incredibly gentle as he dabbed at the red dribbling down her calf.

"You could get lost," he told the now-attentive group. "The weather could change without notice. You could wander away from your party, fall into a ravine and be on your own for days or weeks. Whenever you leave base camp, always take everything you might need to ensure your survival."

"Okay," Sue Ellen murmured, inexplicably sensitive to his touch, "lesson learned."

"Good."

Uncapping a tube of antiseptic ointment, Goodwin smeared cream on the cut before bandaging it with a fresh gauze pad and strips of cloth tape.

"Thanks."

She started to ease her leg off his knee. He clamped a fist around it to hold it in place.

"Second rule of survival. Which is…?"

His glance went around the group. Delilah provided the answer.

"I expect he means you need more than gauze to keep out dust, dirt or water teeming with bacteria."

"Right. Whenever possible, seal cuts or open sores."

His first aid kit yielded a transparent adhesive square about three inches per side. Peeling off the back, he positioned the square over the gauze and pressed the edges tight against Sue Ellen's skin.

"There. You're good to go."

"Thanks. Again."

His callused palm slid up the underside of her calf. For a startled moment Sue Ellen thought the man was copping a feel, but he merely lifted her leg and set her boot on the sandy earth. While her skin tingled from his touch, he remained hunkered down, one arm looped across the knee she'd just vacated.

"Saw palmetto berries were a staple of the Creek and Choctaw, who inhabited this part of the country before their forced removal west of the Mississippi."

Carefully, he nudged the spiky frond aside to show a cluster of dark blue berries at the base of the stem.

"Native Americans also dried them for medicinal purposes. They used them to treat a host of problems, including urinary tract infections and a lack of libido."

Brenda giggled. Rose tried to look bored but Sue Ellen noticed the quick glance she aimed at Rafe Smith.

"Saw palmetto extract can be purchased in health stores today," Goodwin continued. "The U.S. Pharmacopoeia lists it as an effective remedy for the conditions I just mentioned, as well as an enlarged prostate gland, bladder inflammation, breast disorders, bronchitis and laryngitis."

Sue Ellen regarded the jagged-edged leaves with new respect.

"You should never take herbal medications except under the supervision of a licensed health-care provider," the chief warned. "But the American Herbal Products Association gives the saw palm a Class One safety rating, which means it's one of the safest natural remedies to use, with rare side effects."

To demonstrate his point, Goodwin tweaked a few berries from the stem and popped them between his lips. An errant and wholly inappropriate thought darted into Sue Ellen's head as she watched his strong white teeth crunch down on the fruit. Sternly, she suppressed the urge to drop her glance below Goodwin's belt and check to see if the berries were having their advertised effect on his libido.

As he shoved to his feet and reshouldered his backpack, she also tried to suppress the still-tingling sensation his hands had left on her bare skin.

Frowning, Sue Ellen fell back into line behind Ev McPhee. What the heck was the matter with her? Why was she still feeling Goodwin's touch? Crash more than fulfilled her needs. His sheer physical perfection made her wish she could paint or sculpt or even model his naked, muscled body in clay. More to the point, his clever hands and mouth could make her alternately growl like a tigress and mewl like a kitten.

So why was she checking out the chief's butt as he resumed his position near the head of the column? And what was with her sudden, acute awareness of the way his wide shoulders and back tapered to a narrow waist?

Okay, she rationalized. All right. No big mystery here.

She was stuck in the woods for three weeks with a prime specimen of masculinity. Said specimen also happened to possess survival skills well beyond those of ordinary mortals.

It was only natural that she'd start to see him as some kind of a super-macho-outdoorsy-caveman-male.

She needed to remember he put on his pants like everyone else, Sue Ellen told herself firmly…and ground her teeth as her gaze zinged to his butt again, causing her to step down hard on Ev's heel.

"Hey, watch it."

"Sorry."

CHAPTER 4

The Blues returned to the campsite in midafternoon tired, hungry, irritable, bug-bitten and scratched from innumerable encounters with branches and brush. Their "short" hike had lasted hours longer than any of them had expected. After prolonged bickering over how to interpret compass headings, they'd followed the wrong trail on the way back and had trekked miles out of their way.

When they finally trudged into camp, they discovered they'd missed lunch and had several hours to wait until dinner. To Sue Ellen's chagrin, the other Blues seemed to blame her for that as well as their other aches and pains. Paul Sr. threw her a nasty look before limping toward his tent.

"Last damn time I'll head into the woods without a long-sleeved shirt and long pants."

"Or with nothin' but birdseed in our packs," young Jackson McPhee muttered. "Now the dining hall's shut down and we don't get no fu— Ow!"

Rubbing the back of his head, he glowered at his older brother. "Okay, okay. We don't get no damn… Hey!" He dodged another blow and pointed an angry finger at Paul Sr. "What's wrong with *damn?* He just said it."

"He can. You can't."

"Jeee-sus!"

Roger and Dylan made no comment, but the librarian's unhappy squint behind his steamed-up glasses spoke for itself. Brenda pinned on a bright smile and tried to smooth things over.

"Well, I had fun, especially when that tree frog dropped on my neck."

Her mother sighed. "You screamed your lungs raw, sweetie."

"Yes, but now that I look back on it, the whole thing wasn't totally gross."

If running around in circles, screeching and beating at her neck with both fists constituted fun, Sue Ellen thought wryly, Brenda had had a blast.

Rose stayed in character and stalked off without a word, leaving Sue Ellen with the two instructors. Rafe tipped a finger to his brow before departing, but Goodwin lingered a few moments. A rueful smile crept into his eyes as he surveyed her scratched arms and the hair she knew was plastered to her scalp like a sweaty skullcap.

"You okay?"

"No, but I'll survive."

"It probably doesn't seem so at the moment, but the Blues did good for their first time out."

"You think?"

The smile deepened, but all he offered was a word of advice. "Be sure and put some antiseptic ointment on those scratches before we fall out for sports."

Sue Ellen's plans for a cooling dip in the stream hit a speed bump. "Didn't we just *do* sports?"

Hiking through the woods was an Olympic event, wasn't it?

"This is a more organized form of activity," Goodwin informed her. "All part of team-building."

"Oh. Good. More fun."

"See you shortly."

Not if I see you first.

Sue Ellen dragged over to her tent and dumped her knapsack on the sandy earth outside the flap. Rose was sitting cross-legged inside, scrubbing off with a moist towelette from her tent mate's personal stash. Help yourself, Sue Ellen thought, forcing a smile.

"Doesn't that aloe feel wonderful?"

No answer.

"I brought some of my favorite skin cream, too. I love the

scent *and* the emulsions." Plopping down, she rummaged through her hoard of unauthorized extras. She found the square jar and unscrewed the black cap with its distinctive Chanel logo. "Want to try some?"

The perfumed scent wafted on the hot air inside the tent, teasing, tempting. Rose hesitated several long moments before she dipped her fingers into the pale pink cream and smoothed it on her forearm.

"Like it?"

A reluctant nod, followed by a grudging comment. "It smells like the flowers my grandma grew in her garden."

At last! A whole sentence! Sue Ellen felt as jazzed as a climber who'd just conquered the first slopes of Mount Everest.

"What kind of flowers did she have?"

"Roses. Lots of them." Eyes closed, the girl sniffed her arm. "Red and pink and yellow."

"Is that where you got your name?"

The dark eyes opened, revealing a glimpse of utter desolation. As quickly as it had come, the emotion fled and left behind a sullen mask.

"Yeah, I guess. Christ, it's like an oven inside this tent." She scrambled up. "I'm outta here."

Rose's brief flash of despair tempered Sue Ellen's triumph. Thoughtfully, she scrubbed her face, neck and arms with a wet wipe. The teen's profile said she'd been taken away from an abusive, crack-addicted mother. So why hadn't the grandmother with the garden assumed responsibility for the girl?

Maybe she'd been too old or infirm. Or dead. Rose had used the past tense to describe her gardening. Maybe she couldn't be located. Or maybe she just hadn't wanted the burden of raising a child.

Something to add to her list of items to ponder regarding the teen, Sue Ellen thought, along with the girl's bruises and her obvious attraction to the macho Rafe.

Scratches tended to, she was indulging in a soothing dollop of fragrant cream when a bullhorn bellowed.

"Yo! All participants! Fall out for flag Frisbee."

What the hell was that?

Figuring she'd learn soon enough, Sue Ellen screwed the top on the cream and fell out.

FLAG FRISBEE, SHE SOON discovered, was a game played with much shouting and running, governed by complicated and seemingly incomprehensible rules.

The object was to get the Frisbee across your team's goal line, but players could only run laterally. To achieve forward movement, they had to zing the Frisbee to a teammate downfield. The other team attempted to intercept the throw or stop the runner by yanking out the long flag stuck in his or her waistband. No physical contact allowed. Supposedly.

The problem was the damned Frisbee never seemed to fly where the adults aimed it and runners often collided in mid-charge. The kids had much better aim, but just when one team thought they'd gained ground, whistles would shrill and the runner would get called back for an infraction of the rules.

Unfortunately, those same rules said every member of the team had to play. Sue Ellen duly rotated in when it was her turn. She rotated out ten excruciating minutes later, huffing like an asthmatic bull.

That was when she discovered the inadvisability of perfumed skin cream when camping in the woods. The cream combined with the sweat she'd worked up to form a fragrant oil slick that attracted swarms of gnats. Within minutes, she was enveloped in a brown cloud. She received little sympathy from her teammates and none at all from Joe Goodwin. Frowning, the chief sniffed the air.

"What did you douse yourself with?"

"My favorite skin cream," she admitted, swatting the air around her.

"Funny, I don't recall adding perfumed cream to the list of essential survival items."

"It was on the supplemental list I put together," she said

with a nonchalance that was spoiled by the gnat that flew into her mouth. Grimacing, Sue Ellen spit it out.

"Okay," she admitted, "bad idea."

"Very bad. You'd better wash the stuff off or you'll provide a feast for more than gnats. And spray on some repellent," Joe added as she departed the field of battle.

That was the difference between him and Crash, Sue Ellen thought wryly. Bill loved to bury his face between her breasts and breathe in the expensive sent of Chanel No. Five. The chief was apparently more into Eau d'Off!

Not that she wanted Joe Goodwin to nuzzle her breasts, she told herself sternly. Or any other part of her anatomy, for that matter.

Granted, his touch had raised a few goose bumps earlier. And she'd entertained a few idle fantasies during the trek back to camp. No big deal, and certainly nothing to get excited over.

Washed and sprayed, she rejoined the group in time to make another rotation into the game. She was chugging along down the field when the Frisbee sailed in her direction.

"Oh, shit."

Her involuntary mutter got lost amid the shouted exclamations from her fellow Blues.

"Get it, Sue Ellen!"

"Catch it!"

"Jump, girl!"

To her astonishment and the surprise of everyone on her team, she leaped like a bee-stung gazelle and snagged the plastic disk in midair.

"Go, go, go!"

That was Delilah shouting in her ear. Dylan waved wildly from the goal line. Sue Ellen took a bead on his blue T-shirt, dodged a charging defender and darted for a clear spot on the other side of the field.

"I'm on ya," Ev shouted, racing alongside her.

He used his bulk to prevent interceptors from snatching the flag fluttering at the waistband of Sue Ellen's shorts. She found open air and let fling. To her joy, the Frisbee sailed right into Dylan's hands.

"Way to go!"

Ev's congratulatory thunk between the shoulder blades propelled her forward another few paces. She managed to morph those steps into a victory dance as the Blues let loose with whoops and cheers that almost made up for the ugly looks they'd given her earlier.

SHE WAS STILL BASKING in the glow of her goal when the Blues went down to defeat at the hands of the Reds, 2 to 3.

"No matter." Ev looped a beefy arm around his brother's shoulders. "We'll kick some serious butt next time."

Jackson grinned up at him, in perfect harmony with his older sibling for once, while Brenda began recounting the near goals she'd made to anyone who would listen. Since she'd come nowhere close to the goal line, no one did. Even Rose unbent enough to give Sue Ellen something dangerously close to a nod of approval as victors and defeated all made for the mess tent.

A tantalizing scent of roasting meat had been emanating from behind the tent throughout most of the Flag Frisbee game. Sue Ellen's stomach had been rumbling for longer than that. Plate in hand, she joined the line while the cook—another Black Shirt with a livid scar running diagonally across his right temple—dished up beans, coleslaw and succulent, sizzling venison steaks.

After the campers hooked their legs over the picnic-style benches and prepared to dig in, however, the cook proceeded to give a detailed lecture on how to trap, kill and gut various wild animals. Sue Ellen's appetite evaporated on the spot.

An hour of free time followed. Sue Ellen grabbed her shampoo, threw a towel over her shoulder and lined up behind several others at the outdoor shower the Black Shirts had rigged beside the stream. The affair consisted of a canvas tarp tied at the four corners to form a water bag. This was hauled up via a rope looped over the branch of a scrub oak with its roots dug deep in the sandy bank. Holes punched in the canvas bag formed the showerhead.

The setup was primitive but a convenient alternative to just plopping down in the stream. Given the total lack of privacy, the males shucked only their boots, socks and shirts. The females showered in T-shirts and shorts, washing themselves and their clothing at the same time.

After the first few bathers' fumbling attempts to work the tarp, the group adopted a buddy system. One person knelt beside the stream to hold the tarp open, one hauled on the rope and one got doused. Sue Ellen emerged from her turn under the bag cool and refreshed.

"Okay, I've got it."

Kneeling on the white sandbar edging the creek, she took her turn at bag filling. The slow-moving stream was ink-black and impenetrable in the shadows thrown as the sun slipped behind the pines. Sue Ellen kept a wary eye out for ripples that might indicate uninvited guests.

"Do you know why the water is so dark?"

She glanced up to find Joe Goodwin minus shirt and boonie hat, with a towel looped around his neck. He'd spoken to the group at large, but his gaze was on the bag lady. *Her* gaze was on his broad expanse of naked chest.

"No idea," Sue Ellen replied.

One of the kids from the Red team supplied the answer. "We read about water color in biology class. The Gulf of Mexico is, like, bottle green 'cause of sea plankton and stuff, but the cypress trees lining the rivers in this part of the South stain them with some kind of acid."

"Good for you," Joe said. "The acid is called tannin. It leaches from tree roots and leaves that fall into the rivers."

Squatting down beside Sue Ellen, Goodwin dipped his hand in the shadowy water.

"The Creek Indians called the river that feeds this stream *oka lusa*, which means water black."

"Yeah," the teen confirmed. "Our teacher said that's where Okaloosa County got its name."

"I didn't know that," Sue Ellen murmured, noting with some interest the way the chief's fatigue pants molded his muscular thighs. Said thighs were only a few inches from hers. Well within nudging distance.

"Most of the place names in this area derive from the Native American tribes living here when the Spanish arrived," Goodwin confirmed. "Pensacola was inhabited by the Panzacolas. Choctawhatchee means 'river of the Choctaws.' The Apalachicolas gave their name to a town, a river and a swamp."

The bloated tarp was hauled upward, spraying the chief

and Sue Ellen liberally as it rose. She shook her hair back and regarded Goodwin with some curiosity.

"I'm impressed. You certainly know a lot about the indigenous tribes of this area. Is that part of your Special Ops training? You guys have to prep thoroughly before going into a forward location, don't you?"

A smile crinkled the skin at the corners of his eyes. She had to admit those eyes were intriguing. Whiskey-brown and honey-gold. Like him, she thought. A raw punch layered with deceptive smoothness.

"Our mission prep isn't quite that extensive," he confessed. "I have a master's in early American history. My thesis dealt with the migratory patterns of hunter-gatherers in the southeastern United States."

Okay, now she was *really* impressed. With his shaved head and Arnold Schwarzenegger physique, Joe Goodwin hardly came across as the scholarly type. Yet she'd learned more about this corner of the world from him in one day than she had in the four years she'd lived here.

"Why did you study hunter-gatherers?" she asked, edging aside to escape the spray from the makeshift shower.

Joe moved with her. The gnarled oak and the deepening shadows gave them an illusion of privacy in the midst of the bustle of the evening.

"Probably because I have some Choctaw in me," he said in answer to her question, "five or six generations removed. Not enough to qualify for the rolls. Or a share of the profits from the Indian casinos sprouting up like weeds back home in Oklahoma," he added with a chuckle.

"Too bad."

"Tell me about it."

The twilight song of crickets and tree frogs surrounded them. The chief's naked chest had to be a fertile field for the mosquitoes buzzing by, but he didn't seem bothered by them. Eau d'Off! Sue Ellen thought as she flicked her towel at one pesky predator. Joe had probably doused himself in it. She had to remember to carry the damned stuff with her at all times.

"That's what spawned your interest in early hunter-gatherers?" she asked, reluctant to end their little tête-à-tête despite the insects. "Your Choctaw heritage?"

"That, and the fact that I was a hunter-gatherer myself for most of my teenage years."

"What, were you an Explorer Scout or something like that?"

"Something like that." His smile twisted into a wry grin. "My mom died when I was a kid. I always figured she did it on purpose to escape my old man. He was the meanest SOB in three states—particularly after he polished off a bottle, which happened about once a week."

He said it so casually, as if living with a drunk was just the luck of the draw.

"I left home when I was fourteen. Haven't been back since."

"What did you do?"

"Drifted, mostly."

"The authorities never placed you in the system?"

"They never caught up with me. I was big and bulked up enough to pass for sixteen, so I worked odd jobs and lived on what I could scavenge until one day in Missoula, Montana, I sat down at a lunch counter next to an air force recruiter. Two days later, I was on my way to basic training."

"Well," Sue Ellen said quietly, "that explains a lot."

"Yeah, I thought it might."

She cringed inside, recalling her earlier suspicions. Goodwin might still stand to make big bucks as program administrator if his STEP prototype spawned spin-offs across Florida or across the country, but she absolved him of designing the training camp solely as a recruitment tool for the military. Obviously, he'd accumulated some hard-learned life lessons he wanted to pass on to these kids.

A mosquito landed on her cheek, generating a quick

slap and a reluctant retreat. "I'm getting eaten alive. I'd better go spritz and spray."

"Steer clear of the perfume."

"Don't worry! I never make the same mistake twice. Except for my choice in husbands, that is."

She started for her tent, then turned back.

"Thanks, Joe. I understand a little better where you're coming from and where you want to go with this program. I also understand why you wanted me to see the operation firsthand."

Not hardly, thought Joe, as he watched her cross the clearing. With her water-spiked hair and wet T-shirt clinging to every curve, she looked more like one of the kids than a high-powered executive.

The coltish teenage girls didn't affect him. He'd put himself in a mental state that blocked any awareness of their budding bodies, and he'd hammered it into his instructors that they'd damned well better do the same.

He hadn't blocked anything concerning Ms. Sue Ellen Carson, however. Joe had been all too aware of the woman beneath the power suit since their first confrontation. Not many top-level government execs came packaged with violet eyes, silky white-blond hair and a set of curves that spelled danger to any male past puberty.

Joe's suggestion to his Washington pal that the chief of the Department of Labor's Pensacola office should personally evaluate his STEP Program had been legit. Not so legit was the mental image he'd formed at the time of Ms. Carson minus the power suit and stripped down to the bare essentials.

Now she was here, on his turf, and Joe was finding the real woman more tantalizing than he'd anticipated. He was also finding it more and more difficult to remember she had a sky-jock waiting for her at the end of Phase One.

Joe knew all about Major Bill Steadman. After his first tussle with the stubborn Ms. Carson, he'd conducted an in-depth recon on his adversary. Sue Ellen and Steadman had been seeing each other for going on a year now. That said a lot in Joe's mind. Any man who hadn't staked a claim after so many months wasn't trying real hard. Nor, apparently, did she want him to.

The knowledge was satisfying on a deep, visceral level that Joe didn't bother to analyze, but he knew he wouldn't do anything with it. Not yet. Certainly not here, with a total lack of anything resembling privacy. Besides, STEP was too important to him to mess around with the woman holding the purse strings on a much-needed infusion of funds for his program.

But afterward, he thought, eying the curve of her butt as

she ducked into her tent. Afterward was a different story. Savoring the anticipation that tightened his groin, he went to take his turn at hauling up the water bag.

CHAPTER 5

As Sue Ellen toweled her wet hair, she puzzled over the enigma that was Joe Goodwin.

Not many junior-high dropouts went on to earn a master's degree in history. Nor did they advance to the rank of Chief Master Sergeant in Special Ops, with unquestioned, life-and-death authority over teams of highly trained troops.

Now Goodwin was giving up that hard-earned authority, relinquishing his rank and prestige, to work with troubled kids. Sue Ellen admired him for that, even if she wasn't yet convinced his program contained the right mix of ingredients. Her aching calf and shoulder muscles added to her doubts.

Grimacing, she rolled her head and neck to loosen the stiffness her backpack had generated. Although she'd emptied half of the pack's contents—disastrously, as it turned out—the damned straps had still gouged into her shoulders.

"You think you're sore now, wait till tomorrow."

She glanced up to find Rose observing her with a sardonic lift of her brow. The teen had taken a turn at the shower, Sue Ellen noted. Her T-shirt clung to her full breasts and slender waist. Her hair lay thick and heavy and dark across her shoulders. Too thick and heavy for this heat.

"I'd just as soon not think about tomorrow's aches," Sue Ellen said ruefully. "These are enough for now." She waited a beat before reaching for her backpack. "I stuffed a clip in here, thinking I might need it to keep my bangs off my forehead. If you want to do up your hair, you're welcome to it."

Finger-combing her tangles, Rose couldn't help but think what a relief it would be to get the wet, heavy mass off her neck. Then she remembered her reason for wearing it down and responded with a sneer.

"Still trying to lighten your load?"

"Nope." Sue Ellen rummaged through the pack. "I learned that lesson. But the clip wasn't on the list of survival essentials, so I figure it can come out. Ta-da! Here it is."

"I don't want it."

"Stick it in your pocket. You might change your mind later."

"I said, I don't want it."

The flicker of impatience that crossed Sue Ellen's face gave Rose a perverted sense of satisfaction. Sooner or later, they all got bent and stopped making the effort. She'd decided years ago that sooner was better. No sense getting her hopes up when she knew damned well she wouldn't fit in. She never had. Never would.

Except once, during that long-ago summer when her mother had dumped her on *her* mother and disappeared. Rose couldn't have been more than two or three at the time. She'd stayed with her grandmother for what was probably only a few weeks, but had seemed like forever. A safe, warm, wonderful forever. The mental images were old now, and so frayed around the edges that Rose only pulled them out when she really, really needed them.

She'd slipped earlier. She hadn't meant to let the scent of Sue Ellen's silky cream stir her precious hoard of memories, didn't know why she'd even mentioned her grandmother. None of her overstressed caseworkers had been able to trace the woman, or said they hadn't. So they'd shuffled her from one foster home to another.

Some placements hadn't been so bad. One couple had even made adoption noises until he lost his job and their marriage started to unravel along with their finances. Two homes Rose had run away from. This last one…

Her jaw locked. She had three weeks to plan her escape, she reminded herself grimly. Three weeks to figure a way out of the hell her life had become.

"Rose?"

Startled, she blinked and saw Sue Ellen half rising, concern etched in her face.

"Are you all right?"

No! How could I be?

She swallowed the furious retort and spun on her heel. Fat, stupid Brenda made the mistake of crossing her path as she stalked through the enveloping darkness.

"Hey, Rose. Jackson just told me he smuggled in his iPod. He's got some great videos on it. Do you want to…?"

Rose shoved past and left the twit flapping her metal mouth to thin air.

She moved fast, craving space and solitude and the protective shelter of darkness. When she spotted a dim figure leaning against a tree at the edge of the clearing, she cursed and almost changed direction. Then a match flared, a dark head bent and the brief glow outlined Rafe Smith's profile.

Instantly, another emotion piled on top of the others roiling around in Rose's chest. This one she understood. This one she could handle.

Her angry stride slowed to a saunter. Her hips took on a seductive sway. Tucking her hands in the back pockets of her shorts to give Smith an eyeful of chest, she sniffed the sweet aroma of the cigarillo he'd just lit.

"Smells like a Diablo," she commented. "The rum they soak the tobacco in gives it such a distinctive flavor."

"You know your cigars."

"Some," she said with a shrug.

Actually, it was more than some. The crowd she hung with after school made an art of stuffing thin cigarillos with weed to produce nice, fat blunts. Rose had only lit up once. The damned thing had made her so dizzy and sick she puked all over herself. She'd breathed in enough secondhand joy smoke since that ignominious incident, however, to recognize the flavors.

"Got one for me?"

"In about three or four years."

She couldn't see his expression in the dark, only the red tip of his cigarillo, but the amusement lacing his reply brought her chin up.

"Don't let the date on my birth certificate fool you. I've been around."

"I'll take your word for that, *chica*."

She didn't like the gentleness that came into his tone any more than she had the amusement. She wasn't a child, for God's sake. She'd pretty much bypassed that state completely. To prove the point, she sashayed closer. Her right breast brushed his arm. Her voice dropped to a husky murmur.

"Want to take a little walk?"

"I think you missed the point of the Chief's introductory speech this morning. We're here to advise and instruct. *Only* to advise and instruct."

"Okay, so instruct. You could teach me about the stars. The Big Dipper and all that shit." Her fingers tiptoed up his forearm. "Or whatever else came to mind."

"No can do, Rose. Tonight or any other night."

He said it so calmly, so evenly, without the faintest hint of regret. Pride wouldn't allow her to let him see how much his refusal riled.

"Too bad," she said with a nonchalant toss of her still-wet hair. "Guess I'll have to find someone else to see stars with."

"Guess so."

The cigar tip glowed. Sweet, rum-flavored smoke curled through the darkness.

"Just be sure you check for poison ivy before you stretch out to look at the stars."

He was laughing at her! He was just leaning against that damned tree, puffing on his cigar, and laughing at her.

Furious, Rose was tempted to reach out, grab his balls and see how funny he thought *that* was.

"Don't do it."

The soft warning jerked her head up. What was he, psychic or something?

"Do what?" she taunted, testing her limits.

"Whatever you had in mind." He took another long drag. "This is only your first night in camp. You've got a long stretch ahead of you. No sense complicating things or making the whole STEP experience tougher than it needs to be."

"Tougher on me, or on you?"

"On anyone." The chromium dial of his watch lit briefly. "The chief is giving a talk on ways to purify drinking water at 2100. It's a mandatory lecture, one you don't want to miss. You'd better…"

The blare of a bullhorn cut him off.

"Attention all Reds, Blues and Yellows. This is your two-minute call to report to the mess tent."

Rose debated for several moments. The stubborn side of her, the side that more often than not prompted her to do exactly the opposite of what someone told her to, wanted to stalk into the woods. Except the night had grown dark as hell and she wasn't sure she could find her way out again.

She settled for flipping Smith off and putting everything she had into a hip-swinging saunter. Eat your heart out, pal.

Behind her, the cigar tip flared a sudden, scorching red.

W'UD YOU'D SAY, W'UD *you'd do*
   To make me wanna ride a ho like you?

The hip-hop blasting through the bullhorn jerked Sue Ellen from total unconsciousness. Bolting upright on her bedroll, she butted heads with her similarly startled tent mate.

"Watch it!"

Rose's snarl barely penetrated the raucous din. Bumping knees and elbows with the teen, Sue Ellen struggled to peer through the zippered screen of the tent.

A single light penetrated the murky darkness outside. Beneath it stood Chief Goodwin. He held the bullhorn in one hand, something small and indistinguishable in the other.

I'm king a da streets, badder than your old man
Shake that booty, ho. Come get it while you can.

Wincing, Sue Ellen dropped onto her elbows. She had just clapped her hands over her ears when—mercifully!—Goodwin's gravelly voice replaced that of the rapper.

"Mornin', folks. That wake-up came to you compliments of Jack McPhee, who brought his iPod to camp with him. You'll be happy to hear it's got over a gig of memory. Holds two thousand plus songs."

Muffled mutters and curses issued from the huddle of tents, echoing Sue Ellen's groan.

"Loosening-up exercises in fifteen minutes," Goodwin announced. "Breakfast after. Morning trek to follow that."

Flopping down onto her belly, Sue Ellen gave another groan. The precipitous movement nixed any thought of skipping the exercises. She ached in places that had never ached before. Hopefully, a session of stretching and bending would get the kinks out.

It did, much to her relief. Feeling almost human, she scooped scrambled eggs, fried ham and toast onto her plate and joined her fellow Blues.

"Got room for one more?"

"Sure."

Brenda's mom scooted along the bench. Her daughter greeted Sue Ellen with a rubber-filled smile. Polite, earnest Roger Bendix offered to fetch a cup of coffee for her. Paul Sr. sent the younger McPhee brother a sour look and wanted to know what Sue Ellen thought of the wake-up call. Noting Jackson's quick scowl, Sue Ellen opted for diplomacy over truth.

"It got us all up."

The truck driver forked his ham. "I hope to God we don't have to block out that racket every damn morning."

Roger returned with Sue Ellen's coffee in time to catch the comment. Blinking owlishly behind his glasses, the librarian countered with a suggestion.

"Why don't you try listening to it instead? There's a reason rap is now the top-selling music form in the world."

"Yeah, kids buy it because they know their parents hate it."

"It's more than just an expression of individuality." Wiggling onto the bench beside Dylan, Roger nudged up his glasses with a bent knuckle and surprised everyone with a scholarly defense of hip-hop.

"The gangsta style that became so popular in the early nineties was a very real, very significant social commentary on the widespread unemployment and prison experience of so many ghetto youth. It's become more commercialized since then, but still resonates with urban youth. If we listen to the themes underlying the words and music, maybe we'll understand what young blacks and Asians and Latinos think and feel."

Obviously unconvinced, Paul Sr. shook his head and jerked a thumb at his son. "Hell, I can't even figure out what *this* one thinks or feels."

Roger pursed his lips primly. "You make my point."

The elder D'Raggio crinkled his shaggy brows into a scowl, obviously trying to decide if he'd just been insulted. Before he could make up his mind, Jackson McPhee entered the fray.

"What I want to know is who the f—" He dodged a blow, glared at his brother and set his jaw belligerently. "What I want to know is who told the chief 'bout my iPod."

His accusing look zinged to Brenda, who issued instant denials. No one at the table believed her.

"God!" Disgust written all across her face, Rose threw a leg over the bench. "What a bunch of losers. And we're all stuck here together for another twenty days?"

Her abrupt departure left a strained silence in its wake. None of the Blues looked at one another, but Sue Ellen guessed they were all sharing the same thought. The brief burst of teamwork that had resulted in two goals in last night's game of Flag Frisbee hadn't survived morning wake-up.

"Rose has a point," she said after a moment. "We can do better than this. We *have* to, or the next few weeks will be pure misery."

Brenda's mom added a quiet endorsement. "I agree. We're here. Let's get the most from the experience—and from one another."

The elder McPhee brother hunched his massive shoulders. "How do you propose we work together when none of us knows squat about this wilderness-survival business."

Delilah's hands fluttered. She was a small woman, much thinner than her daughter, but with the same wavy blond hair and china-blue eyes.

"I don't know. Maybe we should do what Roger suggested and listen. Just listen. To the chief, to our instructors." Her glance went around the table. "To one another. Seems to me the collective wisdom of ten people ought to be enough to get us all over unfamiliar ground."

Sue Ellen felt a renewed respect for the mother of three. So, apparently, did the others at the table. With mutters of agreement, they broke to prepare for their second excursion into the wilds.

A HALF HOUR OUT FROM CAMP, the whole team was swimming in sweat and the drag of Sue Ellen's backpack had her sore muscles burning. Wincing, she rolled her shoulders.

Ev glanced around at that moment, caught her expression and came to a dead stop. "How dumb are we? We should redistribute the loads so the biggest and strongest carry the most."

Sue Ellen's negative was swift and instinctive. She hadn't climbed the corporate ladder by failing to pull her weight.

"I'm okay."

"No, you're not. Your face is as red as the Alabama secondary when I bust through their line. Here, let me carry some of your gear."

"I can manage."

Delilah laid a hand on her arm. "Listen to him."

Flushing, Sue Ellen chewed on her lower lip. The feminism bred into her by years of holding her own in any and all situations warred with common sense. Logic won the day.

"This will probably get me kicked out of WomanPower Inc., but… Thanks."

"You're welcome."

Challenged by their instructors to retrieve lunch from the meandering Blackwater River, the Blues debated the best methodology. The boys wanted to whittle wooden spears and wade in. Roger suggested scooping. The non-fisher persons in the group stayed out of the discussion until Brenda remembered the spool of tensile thread included in the Hiker's Special Sewing and Canvas Repair Kit. The same kits yielded giant safety pins that could double as hooks.

The bubbly blonde basked in the group's approval as they all sat down to thread their lines.

"We need bait," Paul Jr. commented, glancing around, "or something bright and shiny to use as a lure."

With an inward twinge, Sue Ellen rummaged in her pack for her spare camp shirt. "The buttons are brass. We could use those."

"I dunno." Paul Jr. and Sr. exchanged dubious glances. "The water's pretty dark. Worms or grubs would probably work better."

Sue Ellen might have to deal with worms and grubs

before the three weeks were up. Today she went with bright and shiny.

"Tell you what. You guys try worms. Rose, how about you and I go with the buttons?"

The teen's quick acceptance suggested Sue Ellen had finally hit on something they both had in common—an aversion to slimy.

And water snakes, it turned out. By mutual agreement they decided to stick to the bank instead of wading into the shallow water to cast their lines. Rose chose a bend in the river marked with a half-submerged log. Another log provided convenient seating on dry land.

"Here goes," Sue Ellen muttered, making sure her tent mate was clear before whirling the weighted line like a lasso. The glittering brass button spun through the air and entered the water with a small plop. Rose's hit a moment later.

After that came long stretches of silence broken only by the lazy slap of the river against its bank. The trees arched overhead, forming a dense green canopy that shut out the sun but not the heat. Sweat trickled between Sue Ellen's breasts. The dark water swirled by. She was dozing, half asleep, when the line almost jumped out of her hand.

"I've got something!"

Scrambling to her feet, she hauled her line in hand-over-hand. Rose crowded her shoulder to offer advice and encouragement. They were both almost dancing with excitement when lunch flopped onto the riverbank.

Before they could decide what to do with it, Rose's line went taut. "Hey! I've got a hit, too."

The commotion drew the others. Rose landed her catch to a chorus of shouts and encouragement. All ten Blues gathered around to admire the flapping, flopping fish.

"What are they?" Sue Ellen asked.

Joe supplied the answer, his whiskey eyes gleaming with approval. "Shellcracker bream."

"Are they good to eat?"

"Very good."

A wide grin spread across Rose's face. For the first time she looked like the teenager she was.

"Okay, team. Sue Ellen and I caught 'em. The guys can clean 'em."

Thrilled that the teen had identified herself as part of the group, Sue Ellen shot Joe a quick glance. He returned the look with a small smile.

SWEATY AND EXHAUSTED and pretty pleased with themselves, the Blues straggled back into camp several hours later. The men dumped their packs, peeled off their shirts and hit the shower/stream. The women went in fully clothed.

Sue Ellen took her turn at tarp-filling and hauling. She half hoped Joe would join her at the stream as he had the day before. When he didn't, disappointment rippled through her.

Sluiced off and rejuvenated, she reattached several much-scrubbed brass buttons to her camp shirt. She'd lost one to a broken line and one to a bad throw, but the remaining three covered the essentials. Tying the shirttails at her waist, she joined Rose for the short walk to the mess tent.

Her ridiculous sense of anticipation gave her pause. Just what—or who—was she so eager to see?

The answer came toward them from the opposite direction carrying a full backpack.

"Are you off again?" Sue Ellen asked Joe in surprise.

"I have to do a little night recon to prepare for tomorrow's exercise."

"That sounds scary," Rose commented.

His smile slipped out, crinkling the skin at the corners of his eyes. "It won't be too bad. See you later."

Rose nodded. Sue Ellen struggled with another, thoroughly annoying stab of disappointment.

CHAPTER 6

The days soon settled into a familiar routine. Up with the dawn, calisthenics to loosen stiff muscles, longer and longer excursions into the woods. Lunch beside a stream or hunkered down on fallen logs, with a menu of fruits, nuts, game or fish scavenged by the team under the watchful eyes of the Black Shirts. At least one hour of team sports every afternoon or evening. A lecture or demo after supper.

For those with the stamina, there were late-night gatherings in the mess tent or around a campfire. Sue Ellen attended a few sessions, but started cracking yawns within a half hour or so. She never had any problem staying awake into the small hours at home, especially when she was dealing with a full briefcase of work. Or when Crash stopped by. But then at home she didn't spend hours tramping through woods or chasing a Frisbee down a field.

Actually, she acclimated to the physical demands much sooner than she expected. By the end of the first week, her shoulders adjusted to the drag of her backpack and her calves didn't burn as much. She also acquired a glorious tan that would have cost her megabucks at the spa. With the tan, unfortunately, came unwanted calluses from her boots that would require some serious pedicuring once she returned to civilization.

The most difficult adjustment for Sue Ellen was the lack of privacy. After years of living on her own and loving it, she chafed at the enforced intimacy with a tent mate she still had to force into conversation. She also learned a good deal more about her fellow Blues' personal habits and idiosyncrasies than she'd anticipated or desired. Like Dylan's unfortunate tendency to let loose with nose-wrinkling stinkers with little or no warning. And Brenda's habit of babbling nonstop when she got excited or nervous or both. And the abstract texts Roger Bendix quoted with annoying frequency.

At the same time, she also learned to appreciate their individual strengths. Delilah's unfailing patience when dealing with her daughter won Sue Ellen's respect. Ev's deep, if heavy-handed love for his younger brother came through with every thump. The dry and completely unexpected sense of humor Paul Jr. demonstrated once the other Blues got him out from under his father's shadow.

By contrast, the instructors remained pretty much on the periphery so as not to influence each group's dynamics.

Their only real interaction with the teams came during scheduled activities. Even then, they rotated regularly among the Reds, Blues and Yellows to share their individual areas of expertise.

And experts they were! Joe Goodwin was the acknowledged authority on getting from point A to point B under any and all conditions. Sue Ellen learned more about map orientation, compasses, azimuths, triangulation, packing techniques and land travel over rough terrain than she'd ever imagined she could absorb. Rafe Smith proved to be uncanny when it came to constructing shelters from seemingly bare earth. He also demonstrated how to build fires using a wide assortment of the most unlikely materials. The other instructors imparted information on ground-to-air distress signals, river navigation, cloud formations as indications of potential weather, emergency medical aid and extracting life-saving liquid from an astonishing variety of sources.

The teams got to field-test their accumulated knowledge toward the end of the second week when they set out on a four-day, three-night expedition. Rose's lower lip poked out when Rafe Smith joined the Yellow team, but Sue Ellen couldn't deny a little dart of pleasure when Joe Goodwin and another Black team member joined the Blues.

The first two days of the expedition involved long treks and direct application of the team's hard-learned skills.

Evenings they gathered around a smoky campfire that kept the worst of the mosquitoes at bay. Acclimated to the heat and humidity now, Sue Ellen slept the sleep of the dead all through the dark hours of the night.

Disaster didn't strike until late on the third day.

It happened while they were fording a branch of the Blackwater on their return trek to base camp. As taught, they scouted upstream and down for the best crossing site.

"This looks good," Roger said, squinting at a spot where the water broke into three channels. The Blues had learned the hard way that crossing several smaller channels was considerably easier than tackling the wide, dark river.

"Do you think so, Rog?" Young Dylan's eyesight was better than his mentor's. Pointing, he directed the librarian's attention to the far bank. "Look how the water swirls around those half-submerged rocks. Could be swift currents there. And the rocks will be slippery."

It was a measure of how far they'd all come that the group accepted the teen's assessment without question or debate. Joe and the other Black Shirt kept their own counsel, but Sue Ellen could see a hint of approval on the chief's rugged face as he observed their interaction.

"Good eye," Roger commented, hitching his pack higher on his thin shoulders. "Let's try farther downstream."

They eventually chose a spot marked by several sandbars,

which should have made the crossing a snap. Still, they'd learned enough by now to take all necessary precautions.

To lessen the current's pull, they removed their outer garments, rolled the items up and strapped them atop their backpacks. Boots stayed on to protect their feet from rocks and provide better footing. Ropes looped each team member together to prevent any single individual from being swept downstream by the dark, swirling water.

The strongest Blue—big, hulking, broad-shouldered Ev—went first. With a long pole to anchor himself against the current, he waded in and headed downstream at a forty-five-degree angle. His brother went next, then Joe. Sue Ellen, Rose, Paul Jr. and Paul Sr. followed, with Brenda, Delilah and the second Black. Dylan and Roger brought up the rear.

The water felt blessedly cool as it swirled around Sue Ellen's knees. She welcomed its wash when it rose to her waist and didn't mind at all when it lapped over her breasts. By the time she reached the first sandbar, she'd shed at least a pound of sweat and dirt.

Matters got dicey after the sandbar, however. Ev, as first off, plunged instantly to mid-chest. Sue Ellen, the shortest, had to use the rope as a lifeline. Scissor-kicking, she got through the current and around the large, half-submerged boulder some yards from the bank. She was huffing her way out of the water when Paul Sr. swore sharply.

"Dammit!"

Sue Ellen spun around just in time to see the burly truck driver go under. His weight dragged the girl roped behind him down, too. She sank out of sight with a startled *glub*.

"Brenda! Baby!"

Frantic, Delilah trod water and yanked on the rope linking her to her daughter. Paul Jr. did the same for his father.

Brenda surfaced first. Sputtering and gasping, she shook like a wet, oversize puppy in a futile attempt to get her hair out of her face. Paul Sr. shot out of the water a second later. His panting son strained to hang on while the father flailed wildly and fought to regain his balance.

"Dad! You okay?"

"Yeah, yeah. I slipped on the damned rocks. But when I went under, I think…"

Contorting, he strained to view the back of his arm. Even from where she crouched on the bank, Sue Ellen could see the gaping wound.

"Jesus, I think something bit me."

"Bit you? Stay right there!"

Paul Jr. kicked over to his dad. The burly teen's eyes were wide, his face tight with worry, yet his voice was astonishingly steady as he hooked his shoulder under his father's good arm.

"Okay, just stay calm. I've got you."

"I can make it."

"No! Don't try to swim!" Paul Jr.'s adolescent muscles bunched with iron determination. "Let the others pull us in."

Ev was already hauling on the ropes, assisted by a grim-faced Joe. Jackson, Rose and Sue Ellen scrambled to help the D'Raggios up the bank, where Paul Sr. sank down, cross-legged and white-faced.

Sue Ellen's heart thumped painfully against her breast-bone when she spotted the blood gushing from the vicious gash. Her mind zinged back to her first day at STEP, when a saw palm had jumped out and attacked her. This slashing cut looked very similar, not like a bite mark at all. She kept silent, however, while Delilah knelt beside Paul.

With her previous nursing experience, the mother of three had evolved as the Blue's natural leader when it came to medical matters, eclipsing even Joe and the other Blacks. Brow furrowed, she probed the wound.

"This isn't a bite," she said after a moment, confirming Sue Ellen's guess.

Not completely convinced, Paul Sr. twisted his arm to view the wound. "So what got me?"

"I don't know." Brenda's mom shared a worried glance

with her fellow Blues. "A cut like this could have resulted from any number of sharp objects. A tail fin, maybe. Or a submerged branch. Or a rusty tin can propelled by the current. I can stitch him up, but he should really get a tetanus shot. I wish I knew what cut him."

Brenda chimed in at that point. "I saw something bright when I went under."

Her mother aimed a swift, warning glance in her direction. "Not now, sweetie."

"I did," her daughter insisted. "I really did. It was wedged against that big rock we had to go around."

"Stop it!" Delilah snapped. "This isn't the time or place for one of your stories."

Brenda's chubby face crumpled, but she held to her guns and met her mom's steely look.

"I'm telling the truth this time. I swear. My eyes were open when Paul dragged me down. I saw something glinting in the water but I was too startled to pay any attention to it."

Delilah hesitated, obviously desperate to believe her daughter.

"You need to trust me on this." Brenda's gaze made a circuit of the group. "All of you."

After a moment of stark silence, Paul Jr. surged up. "I'm going back in. If there's something there, I'll find it."

"I'm with you," Ev announced, heaving to his feet.

Sue Ellen's mind was already racing with the logistics of getting the two males back out of the swirling current.

"Com'on, Roger. We'll rig a safety harness. Dylan, loop one of the ropes around a sturdy tree. We can use it as an anchor."

"I'm on it."

Rose jumped up as well. "The guys will need a flashlight to see in that dark tannin. I'll get the one in my backpack."

Leaving Brenda to assist her mother, the others sprang into action. It was only as Paul Jr. and Ev prepared to plunge back into the river that Sue Ellen realized neither Joe Goodwin nor his fellow Black had uttered a single word of guidance or advice. The Blues had developed their plan of attack and coordinated the action on their own.

The realization generated a fleeting moment of satisfaction mixed with a healthy dose of doubt. Were they doing the right thing by letting Paul Jr. and Ev muck around in the dark water?

With an impatient toss of her head, Sue Ellen shelved the thought. Joe would have stopped them—or elected to go in himself—if he considered the risk too great. Still, as she hooked Ev into the hastily rigged harness, she couldn't restrain a quick glance over her shoulder.

Joe's nod signaled both approval and reassurance. It also brought home just how damned good he was at this instructing business. His years of Special Ops training and experience more than qualified him to take the lead in any crisis situation. Yet he'd reined in his own instincts and let them make all the decisions.

Whipping her glance back to the unfolding drama, Sue Ellen helped play out the rope attached to the two harnesses. Chest high in the water, Ev used his bulk to direct the main force of the current away from Paul Jr. Groping cautiously around the boulder, Paul flicked on the waterproof flashlight looped around his wrist, dragged in a lungful of air and sank out of sight.

Sue Ellen and the rest of the Blues held their collective breaths until he resurfaced. The grim determination on his face told them he'd struck out on his first try. Gulping in more air, he went under again.

It took four tries before a seemingly disembodied arm shot out of the water, waving wildly. Paul Jr.'s head joined his arm a second later.

"Got it."

Whatever "'it" was.

Anxious to find out, Sue Ellen and the others helped him and Ev clamber back onto the bank. The shiny, triangular-shape object the teen deposited at his father's side defied immediate definition. Grunting, Paul Sr. touched the object with his foot.

"Looks like copper. Beaten copper."

"Beaten is right." Curious, Jackson hunkered down to trace a finger over the odd-shaped piece. "Like someone flattened a penny to a big trapezoid and hammered swirls into it."

"But what's with the slits?" Rose asked. "And that other triangle sticking out on one side?"

"I do believe…" Dropping down beside Jackson for a closer look, Roger adjusted his glasses. "Yes, I'm quite sure this might be a funerary mask."

"Say what?" The younger McPhee snatched his hand away. "You mean, like, in dead people?"

"Exactly."

"Ya gotta be friggin' kidding me."

Nose scrunched in disgust, McPhee swiped his hand on his wet jeans. Paul Sr. didn't look any happier than the teen.

"That's what sliced into me?" the injured trucker growled. "A damned mummy's mask?"

"I don't think you need to worry," Roger assured him. "I would guess this is quite old. Ancient, in fact. The body the mask graced would have long since rotted away."

"Ewwww."

Brenda and Rose chorused their response to that bit of information in unison. Grinning at the girls' reaction, Joe confirmed Roger's supposition.

"He's right. The mask looks Olmec in origin, most likely traded from the Mayans in Mexico."

The Mayans?

Sue Ellen eyed the piece with renewed curiosity. Her knowledge of Native American cultures was sketchy at best, but even she knew the Mayan empire flourished for thousands of years, reaching its apex long before the Spanish conquistadores arrived.

"No one's quite sure about the exact purpose of thin, decorative copper face shields like this one," Joe continued. "One school of thought holds that they fit over heavier stone or jade funeral masks. Another is that the aristocracy wore them on ceremonial occasions. The richer and more powerful the owner, the more elaborate his masks."

"Cool," Dylan murmured. "So this came from, like, a king's grave?"

"Possibly."

Excited by the find, Roger swiveled on his heel and surveyed the immediate area. "The river undoubtedly changed course over the years. Perhaps it eroded the bank, exposed the burial site." His voice spiraled with enthusiasm. "We should look and see if we can locate it and report the find to—"

"Screw that!" A wet, bristling Paul Jr. gripped his father's shoulder protectively. "We need to hustle Dad back to base camp so he can get the tetanus shot Delilah talked about."

"Yes, of course." Abashed, Roger reordered his priorities. "Sorry, D'Raggio. Can you walk, or did the loss of blood make you weak? If so, we'll build a litter to transport you."

The Blues nodded their agreement. It said wonders for how far they'd all come, Sue Ellen thought with a small jolt of amazement, that no one on her team appeared the least daunted at the prospect of constructing a litter and hauling the heavy-set Paul Sr. back to camp.

"I can walk," the patient asserted gruffly, seeming embarrassed now by all the fuss. "If we take it slow."

"We will," his son promised.

When his dad grunted in response, the Blues pushed to their feet. Roger rose as well, but his gaze lingered on the copper mask.

"That mask is probably quite valuable," he said to the two Pauls. "You should take it with you."

Father and son looked to Joe for guidance. "Can we?"

"You can. Whether you can keep it is another matter. Since this is state land, the law requires you to report any significant historical or archeological finds. If this piece is as valuable as I think it is, the State will probably claim it." His rugged face softened into a smile. "But you two will get credit for the find. If it goes into a museum, which I suspect it will, your names will go with it."

"No kidding?"

The Pauls contemplated their find with some astonishment.

"Well," Paul Sr. said after a moment, "if it goes into a museum, it goes in with all of our names on it. Hoss here couldn't have retrieved it from the river without Ev and the rest of you helping him. Wrap it up," he instructed his son, "and stick it in your backpack."

When the teen started to comply, Paul Sr. stilled him by reaching up and snagging his hand. He had to work for a moment to get out the words, but they finally came.

"Thanks for looking out for me, son."

A flush mounted Paul Jr.'s cheeks. Obviously, shows of affection didn't come easily for either D'Raggio.

"Yeah, well…" Looking acutely uncomfortable, the teen shrugged. "You done it often enough for me."

They left it at that, but the brief exchange tugged at Sue Ellen's heart. If nothing else, she thought, STEP had helped bridge a little of the gulf between father and son.

SHE WAS STILL MULLING over the incident at the river long after the Blues had arrived safely back at base camp. Once there, Paul Sr. received an oral dose of the tetanus vaccine, prescribed by the team's doc over the phone and administered by one of the certified EMT Black Shirts.

Exhausted from their long trek, most of the others

showered, chowed down, reviewed the lessons learned and collapsed in their tents. Sue Ellen had fully intended to do the same, but found herself too restless to sleep. Leaving Rose sprawled facedown on her bedroll, arms flung out on either side, she unzipped the tent screen flap and crawled out.

The scent of the day-old, reheated sludge that passed as coffee drew her to the mess tent. There she found five or six Blacks grouped companionably at one of the tables. With a smile for the guys, Sue Ellen claimed her coffee and would have departed the scene.

"Come join us," Joe suggested.

"You sure? I don't want to interrupt your staff meeting."

"We finished a while ago. We're just shooting the breeze now."

Elbowing the man next to him, he made room for her on the bench.

"That's some find you Blues made today," Rafe commented as Sue Ellen wedged in between two solid walls of muscle. "Joe says he thinks the mask may be pre-Columbian."

"Yeah, we're pretty jazzed about it." She slanted Joe a sideways glance. "I'm even more jazzed at how the experience seemed to close some of the gap between the D'Raggios. Temporarily, anyway."

"They'll have to work to keep it from reopening," the chief agreed. "Won't be easy, but we'll give them some useful tools in the next phases of the program."

"Mmmm."

Fiddling with her coffee, Sue Ellen recalled another moment of stark truth, when Brenda and her mom had looked each other in the eye.

"I see now that's the purpose of Phase One," she said slowly. "It really doesn't have as much to do with survival training as with stripping things down to basics and starting over from there."

"That's exactly the intent," Joe said with a pleased smile. "You broke the code."

"Took me long enough." Her smile matched his. "For what it's worth, you've got my endorsement. I'll send in my recommendation for federal funding as soon as we get back."

The Blacks greeted the quiet announcement with whoops and high fives. After the general jubilation subsided, Joe got serious.

"We should talk about the documentation you'll need to support the recommendation. Want to kick it around now, or are you too tired?"

"Me? Tired? After hiking a mere fifteen miles today? Naaaah."

OKAY, SO SHE'D LIED. Just a little.

When Sue Ellen departed the mess tent some time later, her tail was dragging.

And no wonder, she mused, batting aside a pesky mosquito. This had been a pretty eventful day. Aside from the Blues' accomplishments as a team, they'd made personal advancements as well. The two Pauls had connected. Brenda and Delilah had shared a moment of blind trust. Ev and his brother were making noticeable progress. The whaps to the back of Jackson's head had diminished in both frequency and volume. Even Dylan and Roger had found areas of shared interest.

So why hadn't she and Rose made the same progress?

Her satisfaction fading, Sue Ellen reassessed her strategy for dealing with the teen. Maybe she needed to stop pussy-footing around. Come right out and ask about the bruises that had now faded to faint smudges.

She'd backed off up till now. She'd like to think at least part of her reticence stemmed from respect for Rose's privacy, but she knew darn well it was due to her tent mate's stubborn refusal to engage in anything resembling a serious conversation. With less than a week left in camp, however, it was time to reengage.

Fueled by a renewed determination, Sue Ellen tugged on

the zipper of the screen flap and knelt to crawl in. It took a second or two for her eyes to adjust to the gloom, another to see the patch of dirt previously occupied by Rose—and that her bedroll was now bare.

CHAPTER 7

Her heart in her throat, Sue Ellen conducted a quick sweep of the darkened camp. There was a chance, a slim chance, that Rose had tired of sharing a tent and had strung up a mosquito net to sleep under the stars.

When her hasty search revealed no trace of the girl, she knelt at the entrance to the tent next to hers.

"Delilah!"

Either the older woman's nursing or mother instincts operated on full alert—Sue Ellen's urgent whisper roused her instantly. Blinking owlishly, she stuck her face up to the screen.

"Whazzup?"

"Have you seen Rose?"

"Not since dinner. Why?"

"She's not in our tent. Her bedroll and backpack are gone, too."

Yanking down the zipper, Delilah thrust aside the flap and squinted at the next tent, as if that would make the missing girl materialize.

"Did she say anything to you at dinner?" Sue Ellen asked. "Or maybe Brenda?"

"No, we…"

Her breath catching, Delilah shot a glance at her softly snoring daughter. Doubt and dismay colored her voice.

"Oh, no! She wouldn't. Not again."

Sue Ellen's stomach dropped. "She wouldn't what?"

"There was an incident with one of the neighbor's kids. Last year. Brenda convinced her to run away, gave her some money. Her parents found her at the bus station, but…"

Her voice trailing off, Delilah reached into the tent and shook her daughter's shoulder.

"Brenda. Sweetie. Wake up."

The girl mumbled an inarticulate protest and buried her face in her bedroll.

"Wake up!"

"Ten more minutes, Mom."

The plea was muffled and fuzzy and more than a little surly, but Delilah was relentless.

"I want to talk to you. Now."

Shaken out of her usual bubbly cheerfulness, the teen propped herself up on an elbow and snarled at her mother. "Okay, okay! I'm awake."

"Do you know where Rose is?"

"Huh?"

"Rose. Do you know where she is?"

"Isn't she in her tent?"

"No, she isn't."

Sue Ellen leaned inside the opening, adding her voice to the inquisition. "Did Rose talk to you tonight? Say anything about leaving camp?"

The teen plucked at her bedroll, opened her mouth, shut it again. The possibility she might embellish on the situation or flat-out lie elicited a sharp demand from Sue Ellen.

"Be straight with me, Brenda! I need a yes or no. Do you know where Rose is?"

"No."

"Honestly?"

"Honestly."

"Okay."

Sue Ellen backed out of the tent, her stomach now churning with worry and the acid of too much coffee. Added to the mix was a roiling sense of shame at her failure as a mentor and a friend.

So much for the resolutions she'd made just moments ago, she thought on a wave of bitter self-disgust. Too little, and way too late.

Joe was still in the mess tent with his staff. His calm response to the news that Rose appeared to have decamped went a long way to soothing Sue Ellen's snapping nerves.

"If she has left, she couldn't have gone far. We'll find her." Swinging a leg over the bench, he mobilized his team. "Harper, you run the north perimeter. Dodds, Singer, Jordan, take the west, south and east respectively. Talbot and Robinson, conduct a tent-by-tent check of the Reds and Yellows. Smith, you come with me to interrogate the Blues."

"I've already asked Brenda and her mom," Sue Ellen informed the two men as they accompanied her across the clearing. "Neither of them saw or heard anything."

When the trio reached the Blue area, they found Brenda and Delilah and the rest of the Blues up and dressed.

"We've got some news."

The guarded note in Delilah's soft voice twisted Sue Ellen's insides. "What?"

"Rose took the mask."

"Are you sure?"

She swung toward Paul Jr., who confirmed the mask was missing.

"After I showed it to everyone earlier this evening, I wrapped it in my spare shirt for safekeeping and stashed it in this box."

Paul Jr. dangled an empty carton, his face a study in disappointment and betrayal. Paul Sr. gave his son's shoulder a consoling squeeze.

"Hoss says Rose went with him to get the box from the mess tent. Said she saw him tuck the mask inside and stick it in a corner of our tent. All she had to do was reach under the canvas and slide it out."

Sue Ellen's guilt kicked up six or seven more notches. Rose had been so desperate to get away she'd lifted what might turn out to be an extremely valuable artifact. All the while Sue Ellen sat swilling coffee and rubbing shoulders with Joe Goodwin and company, completely ignorant of her tent mate's intent.

Okay. All right. Fists clenching, Sue Ellen gave herself a swift, mental kick. She needed to stop with the guilt. This wasn't the time for self-recriminations. Those could come later. Right now she needed to focus all her attention on finding a missing teen.

WITH THE NIGHT HEAVY and close around her, Rose aimed her flashlight at the folded map.

She wasn't lost.

She couldn't be lost.

She'd paid such close attention when Joe showed them how to read the compass. Stood right at his shoulder when he'd had them find the North Star and figure out how to use it to verify course and direction. She'd also highlighted the old logging road on her map.

Map, compass and the stars she glimpsed intermittently through the trees all said she was headed in the right direction. No reason to feel scared or lost. Or so friggin' alone.

She'd been alone before. All her life, really. This time, though, she was taking control. Making the decisions. No more social workers. No more foster homes. No slimy creep spying on her in the bathroom. Or sneaking into her bedroom late at night with a hard-on.

Fury rippling through her, Rose aimed the flashlight at the barely discernible dirt path. If the map was right, if she hadn't followed the wrong track or gotten turned around ass-backward in the dark, she should hit a two-lane paved road by dawn. Then she'd flag down the first vehicle that came along and feed the driver a line of bull about getting lost and separated from the rest of her party. When she reached civilization, she'd hunt down a pawnshop or antique store and sell the copper mask.

She felt bad about lifting the mask. Paul Jr. was a little thick, but okay. She'd seen how finding that bit of metal had puffed him up in his old man's eyes. Still, if the thing was as valuable as everyone seemed to think, it should bring enough to get her to… To…

Somewhere.

Jaw set, Rose trudged through the dark tunnel of trees.

"SHE TOOK THE OLD logging road."

The terse announcement came after the most nerve-racking half hour of Sue Ellen's life. She and the other Blues crowded close while the beefy, bull-necked Black with the incongruous name of Clarence Dobbs made his report to Joe.

"I picked up her tracks about a quarter of a mile down the road. The kid's smart," he added. "She used a tree branch to dust the road behind her. Good thing we didn't get into detailed escape-and-evasion tactics or she would have varied her side-to-side sweep pattern and I might have missed it."

The brief report killed Sue Ellen's stubborn hope that Rose hadn't really booked, that she was only making a plea for attention or trying to put a scare into them. From the sound of it, she'd planned her escape down to the last detail.

"Fire up the ATVs," Joe told his men. "You and Rafe take one, I'll take the other. Rose can ride back with me."

Sue Ellen pushed forward. "I want to go with you."

"We'll be moving fast on a rough, abandoned road. It's best if you stay in camp. We'll bring her back."

She was damned if she was going to sit in camp and twiddle her thumbs. She'd let Rose down enough as it was.

"I'm her sponsor. I want to help find her."

He shot her an assessing glance but didn't waste time arguing. "All right. Put on some protective clothing."

Racing to her tent, Sue Ellen pawed through her gear. She was hopping on one leg, dragging her jeans up the other, when an ATV engine roared to life. A second engine coughed, then gunned impatiently. Shoving her feet into her boots, she snatched up a long-sleeved shirt and jammed on her ball cap.

Mere moments later she was pressed against Joe Goodwin's back, her teeth rattling as they jounced over the pitted track.

ROSE HEARD THE FAINT sounds of pursuit coming at her through the night and spit out a curse. She'd figured they would mount a search. She'd swept that damned tree branch behind her for what felt like hours. She was sure she'd wiped out her tracks, had counted on it taking until daylight for them to pick up her trail. By then, she would've hit the main road.

Throwing a glance over her shoulder, she saw nothing but inky darkness. How close were they? Probably closer than she thought. The trees and scrub brush muffled sounds. Should she duck into the woods now, or try to make the road?

It didn't help that her flashlight beam was growing dimmer by the minute. She could barely see ten steps ahead. Couldn't see at all on either side. The tall pines leaned in on her, forming solid walls of black. She'd learned enough from Joe and Rafe and the other instructors these past two weeks to really, *really* not want to plunge into the underbrush unless she could see where she was going. She didn't need to plow though a patch of poison ivy or smack into a low-hanging branch.

She stood in the middle of the track, unsure, indecisive, until a faint beam of light speared through the pines.

Hell! They were closer than she'd thought.

Her mind shut down. Pure instinct took over. Thinking only of escape, she broke into a run. She made ten, maybe twenty yards, before she shed her backpack and tossed it into the woods. Freed of its heavy weight, she sped down the road.

She didn't see the rut until her foot came down in it. Her boot rolled, her ankle gave an audible pop, and she fell on her face. The thud when she slammed into the ground knocked the wind out of her. Stunned, she lay in the dirt for a moment.

The whine of engines sent her scrambling onto her knees. Grimacing, she pushed to her feet. The pain brought her right back down. It shot up from her ankle in pulsing, white-hot waves that made her spit out a vicious curse.

Gradually, the waves subsided. Rose gritted her teeth. Tried again. Sank back in agony.

She knelt there in the dirt, head bowed, defeat tasting foul in her mouth. Tears burned her eyes, but she blinked them back. She never cried. Not in all the years she could remember. She wouldn't start now. She *wouldn't!*

SUE ELLEN THOUGHT AT FIRST the creature trapped by the spear of the ATV's headlights was a deer or maybe a large dog. Then it lifted its head, showing the pale blur of a face, and shock jolted through her.

That was Rose on all fours, looking as wild and feral as a she-wolf. Understanding hit the next instant.

Oh, God! She was hurt. Something—or someone—had left her crouched and panting in the road.

The raw, primitive urge to punish whoever or whatever had harmed the girl gave Sue Ellen another jolt. Only as Joe throttled back on the controls did the brutal truth strike home.

She had to shoulder the blame for whatever had happened to Rose. As she'd asserted so arrogantly to Joe, she was the girl's sponsor. She'd agreed to assume responsibility for her.

Helluva job she'd done of it so far.

Sue Ellen was off the ATV and running before Joe killed the engine. She crouched beside the girl, not touching her for fear of adding to possible injuries, but scared all over again by the pain carved into her face.

"What happened? Where are you hurt?"

"My ankle. I stepped in a friggin' rut. Otherwise…" Her breath came in short, hard pants. "Otherwise you wouldn't have found me."

"Yes, I would," Sue Ellen countered swiftly. "I would have searched all night. All day. All next week or month or year. As long as it took."

"Yeah, sure."

Rose couldn't be hurting too badly if she could manage that sneer, Sue Ellen thought with relief. On all fours herself now, she got nose to nose with her charge.

"You listen to me, girl. You can't get away from me that easily. I would have searched until I found you."

Rose blinked, shaken out of her pain for a moment by the fierce counterattack. Grimacing, she twisted onto her rear and plopped down in the dirt.

"Why?" she demanded, bristling with doubt and distrust. "What do you care where I go or what I do?"

Sue Ellen had been struggling with the answer to the same question for most of the bone-jarring ride. Why did she suddenly care so much? Was it just a guilty conscience? Unwillingness to admit defeat?

"Because I said I'd mentor you."

That sounded as lame to her as it probably did to Rose, but it was the only answer she had at the moment.

She caught a shadow of movement in her peripheral vision and chopped a hand through the air to halt the two men. Her gut told her this might be her only chance to bridge the chasm separating her from Rose.

"I've done a piss-poor job of mentoring up to now, I grant you, but I'll do better. I promise. You don't even have to meet me halfway. Just accept the fact that I'm sticking with you, whether you want me to or not."

"I don't need you. I don't need anyone."

"Well, you've got me."

Her mouth set in a flat line, the teen shook her head. "I'm not going back there."

"Rose, you have to. It is either the STEP program or a juvenile detention center. All we have to get through is a few more days in camp. Then it's back to civilization and—"

"You're so dense." Scorn dripped from every word. "I'm not talking about camp. That's a piece of cake."

"Then what?"

Her lips clamped shut. Turning her head, she poked a tentative finger at her ankle and grunted. Sue Ellen reclaimed her attention with a hard tug on her arm.

"What, Rose? What aren't you going back to?"

She knew the answer. Deep in her gut. Her grip eased. Her tone gentled. "Tell me."

Rose yanked her arm free and she spat out a response.

"Where I live, okay? I won't go back there. You can't make me."

She lifted her head and included the men standing behind Sue Ellen in her fierce declaration.

"You, either. I'm getting away from him, even if I have to crawl all the way to…to…" Her voice broke, then came back on an angry rush. "To California."

Sue Ellen responded to the ugly truth instantly and without thinking. "Okay. We'll make it happen. You won't have to go back."

"Mind if I take a look at that ankle?" Joe interrupted.

Sue Ellen pushed to her feet, yielding her place to Joe. He hunkered down and opened his first aid kit. With Rafe bathing the scene in bright light from his industrial-strength flashlight, Joe probed Rose's ankle. Her breath hissed in at his touch, but she gritted her teeth and endured the exam without protest.

"I think it's just a bad sprain," he announced after a moment. "We won't know for sure until it's X-rayed. We'll immobilize it for the trip back to camp, then drive into town. Rafe, I'll need those plastic splints."

Left out of the action, Sue Ellen had plenty of time to review her exchange with Rose. She didn't underestimate the difficulties involved in holding to her promise. She was a government employee. She understood bureaucracy. She hadn't reached her current position, however, without learning how to make its ponderous wheels turn.

So she was prepared when Joe finished splinting Rose's ankle. While he packed up his first aid kit, Rafe scooped up the girl and carried her to his ATV. Joe waited until they were out of hearing before turning to Sue Ellen.

"You made a heavy promise to that girl. How do you plan to hold to it?"

"My condo has a spare bedroom. She can stay with me until we sort things out with her caseworker. Afterward, too, if necessary."

Joe didn't pull his punches. "That isn't going to happen. You're single and you work what I'm guessing are long hours. I suspect your job also requires you to travel quite a bit. No judge will let you assume temporary custody for a teen with Rose's record, assuming they don't send her to juvie for trying to run again."

"They won't, if you and I both go to bat for her."

He hesitated, obviously torn. "I don't mind giving her a second chance, but are you sure you want to assume responsibility for her? She needs full-time supervision."

"Right," Sue Ellen fired back. "Like she's getting where she lives now?"

It was on the tip of her tongue to bring up Rose's bruises, but all she had at this point were suspicions.

"All I'm saying is that you need to think this through."

His even tone took the edge from hers.

"I know, I know. Sorry I snapped at you."

She bit her lip, her gaze on the girl Rafe deposited on the seat of his ATV. Various options raced through her mind and soon narrowed to just one.

"Let's get Rose to a doctor. Then I need to make some calls. Sure would be nice if I had my cell phone," she added pointedly as she and Joe headed for the second ATV.

"You can use mine, or a phone at the hospital."

In deference to Rose's ankle, they took it very slow and made every effort to avoid the worst of the ruts. Still, Sue Ellen's heart jumped into her throat when the girl cried out just a few yards down the dirt track.

"Stop! Please! Stop!"

Her anguished plea carried over the whine of the engines. Rafe braked to an instant stop. Joe pulled up next to him.

"Is the ride too bumpy, Rose? If so, we can construct a litter."

"No, I just… I want my backpack. I tossed it into the woods. I think it was right about here."

"Don't worry about it. We'll supply you with whatever you need."

"You don't understand. I took Paul Jr.'s mask. It's in my backpack. I need to return it to Paul."

Sue Ellen had forgotten all about the copper mask but took heart from the fact Rose hadn't left it stashed in the woods, to be retrieved later in another escape attempt.

She also didn't fail to note the hint of shame under the girl's brittle belligerence. It was good to know she had a conscience buried under all that anger and defiance and hurt.

CHAPTER 8

They got Rose back to camp with what Sue Ellen hoped was a minimum of jolting.

The Blues greeted her return with relief and a flurry of anxious questions. The fuss embarrassed Rose, who shrugged aside their questions and returned the mask to the two Pauls with a gruff apology for taking it.

Sue Ellen accompanied Rose and Joe on the long ride back to civilization. The teenager lay stretched across the back seat of the truck cab, keeping her leg elevated as instructed. As Joe concentrated on navigating the dimly lit road, Sue Ellen plotted her strategy.

Once at the ER, the doctor confirmed Joe's diagnosis of a severe strain. "She'll need to keep off it until the swelling goes down," he cautioned.

"We'll RICE her good," Joe assured him. "Rest, ice, compression and elevation," he translated for the two females.

"No hot showers, heat rubs or alcohol for at least twenty-four hours," the doc added.

Rose's glance snagged Sue Ellen's. Their rueful expressions conveyed the same thought. Either one of them would kill for a hot shower. A beer would taste pretty good right about now, too, Sue Ellen thought.

"No aspirin," the doc continued. "It prolongs the edema. I'll prescribe some painkillers if you need them, or you can go with over-the-counter Tylenol or ibuprofen."

"I don't need painkillers," Rose interjected.

"Good enough. Hang loose, and I'll send a tech in to rewrap this ankle."

"Like I'm going anywhere?"

"She's back," Sue Ellen announced to Joe with a grin. "Let me borrow your cell phone. I need to make some calls."

He handed over the instrument and Sue Ellen ducked out of the exam room. She felt like a beetle-browed Neanderthal stumbling out of a cave into a bright new world. One with air-conditioning. Gleaming tile floors. Real, live phones.

Promising herself a visit to a flushing toilet before they departed the hospital, she flipped open the phone. Her first call was to her best friend in the entire universe. Unfortunately, said friend wasn't home. Tapping an impatient toe, Sue Ellen waited through Andi's prerecorded greeting.

"Andi, it's Sue Ellen. I need a favor. A big one. Call me when you get this message. The number is… Hang on."

Jerking the phone away from her ear, she retrieved the number from the electronic directory and recited it. Her second call was to her office. As expected, she got a recording there, too.

"Hey, Alicia, this is your long-lost boss. I want you to schedule two appointments for me. Make them for the day I get back, if possible. The first is with the Escambia County Child Welfare Division. I want to meet with the caseworker assigned to Rose Gutierrez's case. Got that? Rose Gutierrez. The second is with the lawyer who handled my last divorce. Peter Chobanian. His number is in my Rolodex. Any questions, contact me at this number."

Again, she recited the digits.

The most urgent calls made, she tapped the cell phone against her palm. She was about to flip the lid up again when the instrument began to vibrate and almost jumped out of her grasp. Bobbling the phone like a hot potato, Sue Ellen recognized the number flashing across the screen and got it to her ear on the third ring.

"That was quick. Thanks for getting back to me, Andi."

"No problem. Sorry I didn't catch your call. We were out on the deck, crashing after a small cocktail party for seventy or so…which you *swore* you'd help me with, girlfriend."

"Oh, Lord! Was that tonight?"

"It was."

"How did it go?"

"Pretty good, actually. I cornered the chairman of the regional FEMA office, plied him with margaritas and got him to promise to move on our disaster prep funds. That was worth the whole effort right there. We were toasting the victory when you called."

God, what she wouldn't give to be there with Andi and Dave, enjoying the cool breeze off the bay and a nice post-party buzz.

"Speaking of crashing," her friend added, "your favorite Crash is out on the deck with Dave."

With a small jolt, Sue Ellen realized she hadn't thought about Bill Steadman for days.

"Want to say hi?" Andi asked. "I'll get him."

"In a minute. First, I need to ask that favor I mentioned."

"Whatever it is, you got it."

"Don't you want to hear what I want before you commit?"

Andi snorted into the phone. "This from the woman who put her life on hold to baby-sit me through that little bout of *acinetobacter baumannii* last year?"

Sue Ellen preferred not to think of those awful months when Andi had battled the bug she'd brought home from Iraq. The vicious, drug-resistant bacterium had invaded her heart, weakened the muscle and effectively ended her military career. On the up side, it had brought Andi and her ex-husband back together again.

"How do you feel about sullen, uncommunicative sixteen-year-olds?" she asked her friend.

"I don't know. How do you want me to feel?"

"Like you wouldn't mind having one work in your bookstore this summer."

"Okay. I don't mind having one work in my bookstore this summer."

Silly, soppy tears filled Sue Ellen's eyes. With a little hiccup, she swiped a forearm across her face. This business with Rose had gotten to her more than she realized.

"What did I do to deserve you?" she asked Andi, only half in jest.

"Beats me. Care to tell me who I'm hiring?"

"Rose Gutierrez. The kid I'm sponsoring here at camp."

"The same kid who stole the car?"

"She, uh, just borrowed it."

Sue Ellen waited a beat, giving Andi a chance to back out gracefully. When her friend remained silent, she offered a hurried explanation.

"I'm going to see if I can arrange it so Rose stays with me for a few weeks, but I'd can't take more time off work. I don't want to leave her alone and bored during the day."

Or unsupervised.

"Plus, she needs a summer job to complete Phase Three of the STEP program. You'll really help us both out if you can keep her busy."

"No problem. Will I meet her when I pick you up next Saturday?"

"Yes. I'm going to bring her back to my place that day, if I can swing it. I've got to work some legal angles first."

"I have complete confidence in you, girl. Tell her I'm looking forward to having her help out at the store."

Dave's deep voice rumbled in the background. "Tell who?"

"S.E.'s new protégée. She's going to work at A Great Read this summer."

Sue Ellen strained to hear Dave's response. All she got was an indistinct rattle that sounded like someone had opened a refrigerator door.

"Damn! We're out of beer. Sorry, Crash."

Crash evidently wasn't interested in a refill. Eagerness colored his rich baritone as he queried Andi. "Is that Sue Ellen on the phone now?"

"It is. She wants to talk to you."

She did. She really did. A mental image formed of Crash leaning over her, his handsome face smug with the look of someone who's loved and been well loved in return. Smiling and more than a little hot, Sue Ellen waited for him to come on the line.

"Hey, you."

"Hey," she replied, enjoying the sizzle. "How are you?"

"Horny as hell. What about you?"

Laughing, she propped a shoulder against the corridor wall. "Same goes."

"If Andi and Dave weren't standing right here, making no effort to disguise their prurient interest, I'd tell you what I have planned for your homecoming celebration."

"Give me a hint, sweet cheeks. I need something to get me through the next few days."

"Pandas."

"Huh?"

"Pandas."

"Like in furry, black-and-white critters?"

"Yep."

Sue Ellen tried to visualize a situation, involving her, the sexy chopper pilot and pandas. She failed completely.

"Com'on, Crash. You gotta give me more than that."

"I will, as soon as you get home." The teasing laughter left his voice. "I've missed you."

"I've missed you, too. See you soon."

She hung up, a smile on her lips. Bill Steadman was the perfect lover. Charming, funny, terrific in bed. And young.

Sue Ellen peeled off a dozen years whenever she was with him. Figuratively speaking, unfortunately, but there it was.

Still wearing a smile, she turned and found Joe Goodwin waiting patiently behind her.

"The ER tech is almost finished rewrapping Rose's ankle," he explained. "She'll be ready to go in a few minutes. I thought I should let you know in case you want to raid the snack bar or vending machines before we leave."

"To heck with food. I'm hitting the ladies' room. Someone told me it has hot water coming out of this little spigot. And a real, honest-to-goodness toilet. I'll wheel Rose in, too, when she's done."

When she thrust the phone into his hand and headed for the ladies' room, Joe had to fight to keep his expression neutral. The woman had no clue how her soft, sensual "I miss you, too" had ruffled his fur. He felt like a junkyard dog with fangs bared, ready to go for his rival's throat.

That bit about the hot water hadn't helped, either. Like a fool, he'd convinced himself Sue Ellen had actually started to enjoy herself in the environment he considered his natural turf. How stupid was that?

He was crazy to think she'd fit into his world. Crazy to think she'd *want* to. Administering a swift, mental kick in the butt, Joe whirled and strode back to the exam room.

WHEN THE TECH had finished rewrapping Rose's ankle, Sue Ellen broke the news that she wanted Rose to stay at her condo until they worked out other, more permanent arrangements.

"For real?"

"For real."

She hoped that was relief that flickered in the girl's eyes. The emotion came and went so quickly she wasn't sure.

"I also lined you up with a summer job in my friend's bookstore. You'll like her. She's really cool."

This time the emotion was easier to read. Suspicion and wariness locked Rose's face in a frown.

"Why would your friend give me a job? She doesn't know me from squat."

"True, but she knows me. Andi Armstrong and I have been best buds for almost twenty years. You'll like working for her. Won't she, Joe?"

Thus appealed to, the chief added his endorsement. "She's as solid as they come. So is her husband. You won't find a better man to go into the bush with."

Still frowning, Rose picked at the bandage covering one of her skinned knees.

"The people I'm living with, they count on the money

they get from DHS for us foster kids. They won't give it up that easy."

"We won't ask them to. Not yet. All we're talking about right now is a visit. You spending a few weeks with your STEP sponsor so I can help you complete the program."

Sue Ellen couldn't say more until she talked to a lawyer and the caseworker. Time enough to discuss the legalities with Rose once Sue Ellen had a firm grasp of them herself.

"Andi is also mayor of Gulf Springs. I was thinking we could talk to her about our STEP community service project. Something we could do together in the evenings or on weekends."

"You sure you'll have time?" Joe drawled. "Judging by the conversation I overheard out there in the hall, you might be busy nights and weekends."

The comment doused the little sizzle left over from her conversation with Crash.

She wasn't blind, or so full of herself that she'd imagined the unspoken but undeniable tug between her and Joe Goodwin. She knew he'd experienced the same pull she had. It wasn't just the isolated setting or enforced proximity. There was something there…or had been until the phone call a few moments ago.

Now the warmth she'd grown so used to seeing in his eyes

had cooled. She missed it already. Swallowing a twinge of real regret, she shrugged.

"I'll make time."

THE REGRET GREW DURING the last week in camp.

Joe reported Rose's aborted escape attempt but convinced the authorities to allow the teen to complete STEP. He remained as friendly and instructive as ever, but went out with the Reds and Yellows noticeably more often than he did the Blues. If any of Sue Ellen's teammates noticed his absence, they didn't comment on it. They were too busy preparing for the simulated war games that constituted the final test of their newly acquired survival skills.

All members of the team were required to participate. Since Rose had to stay off her ankle as much as possible, the Blues devised ingenious methods of transporting her through almost impenetrable thickets and across rivers. They managed to ambush the Reds and force their surrender. Unfortunately, the Yellows took them down to ignominious defeat not three miles from the objective.

The awards ceremony and graduation banquet to celebrate compleation of Phases One and Two were boisterous affairs. Teams thumped the table and hooted as each participant marched up to receive his or her award. Sue Ellen won the Most-Missed-Frisbees honors. Rose took home the

Fall-Flat-on-Your-Face trophy. Ev and Jackson McPhee shared the Big-and-Little-Tough-Guys prize.

Her sides aching from laughter, Sue Ellen helped Rose hobble back to their tent. The other Blues trailed alongside, relieved the three weeks were over at last but amazed at how fast the days and nights had sped by. Lingering outside their tents, they relived the highs and lows while the mosquitoes attempted to feast on their tanned and toughened flesh.

"Did I tell you guys that Dylan's going to work part-time in the library this summer?" Roger beamed a smile at his protégé.

Paul Sr. laid an arm across his son's shoulders. "I'm going to see if I can get Hoss here on the dispatch desk. I figure he should see the business side of trucking, since he's gonna go to college after high school. Maybe he'll end up being my boss one of these days. Wouldn't that be a kick in the gonads?"

The group agreed with his assessment.

"Speaking of college," Sue Ellen said, "what's the story, Ev? Will the coach let you back into your summer training program?"

"Hope so. I'm the best tackle they got. First, I gotta get Jackson a job."

"I can help there," Delilah volunteered. "Brenda's going to work at the hospital. I think I can get Jackson on there, too.

It doesn't pay much," she warned the younger McPhee. "Just minimum wage. But you'll learn a lot and be helping people."

"Sick people," he said doubtfully, then dodged a thump to the back of his head. "I guess I kin do it if Brenda kin."

The bubbly blond turned to the girl at Sue Ellen's side. "What about you, Rose? Want to join Jackson and me at the hospital?"

"Sue Ellen got me a job in her friend's bookstore."

"Oh. Okay." Brenda sent a hopeful glance around the group. "Maybe we can all get together sometime? Have, like, a reunion or something."

The Blues made universal murmurs of assent, but no one picked up the ball until Sue Ellen reminded them of the community-based project required in Phase Four.

"There's nothing that says we can't do a project together, as a team."

Paul Sr. rubbed his nose. "I dunno about that. I'm on the road a lot. Ev here might be in training. You have this big, important government job. Roger and Delilah have responsibilities, too. How do we get around everyone's schedule?"

"We work at it," Sue Ellen said firmly. "Together. Just like we did these past three weeks."

Nodding, Roger knuckled his glasses higher. "I'll take on the challenge of setting up the first meeting. I suggest we bring ideas for possible projects and go from there."

"I got one," Paul Jr. put in. "Dad and I are going to turn the copper mask over to the state, like Joe said we should. Maybe we could, you know, help them research it or something."

"Sounds like a plan to me." Ev's friendly slap on the back propelled the librarian forward a few paces. "I can make it work if the rest of you can."

Sue Ellen couldn't believe how much the prospect of reuniting with her fellow Blues buoyed her. It seemed to have the same effect on the others. Considerably cheered, they dispersed to their tents to pack their meager possessions.

She stood patiently, swatting at mosquitoes while Rose hopped, dipped and maneuvered into their tent for the last time.

Thank God!

Tantalized by visions of foaming bubble baths and flickering, perfumed candles, Sue Ellen jumped when a voice came out of the darkness.

"Congratulations."

Joe materialized a moment later. His smile generated a small flutter under her ribs.

"The Blues just aced the team-building phase of the program."

"We did, didn't we?"

Ridiculously proud of her team for deciding to stick

together for the duration of STEP, Sue Ellen returned his smile.

"I have to admit, there were a few moments I wasn't sure we'd make it through any phase."

"You did fine. All of you."

She basked in his quiet praise and made a mental note to share it with the other Blues.

"I know it wasn't easy for you," he added after a moment. "I dragged you into STEP against your will, with next to no notice. Thanks for being such a good sport about it."

"You're welcome. For what it's worth, I think you've designed a great program. I know I certainly learned a lot. About myself, mostly, and what I'm capable of."

"So did I."

"And here I thought you Black Shirts already knew everything," she teased. "What'd you learn, Joe?"

"That I'm not above wanting to poach on another man's territory."

"Excuse me?"

"You heard me."

Her jaw dropped, then closed with a snap. "If you're referring to the conversation you overheard at the hospital…"

"I am."

"Then you need to know I'm not now nor have I ever been any man's 'territory.'"

"Sure sounded as though someone has staked a claim."

"Oh, for Pete's sake! What century are you living in?"

"Good question. I've been struggling with the answer for the past week."

Joe had also been struggling with what he knew were antiquated notions of honor and fair play and the brotherhood of arms.

The military constituted his family. His only family. Sue Ellen's sky jockey wore the same uniform he did. The unwritten rules said you didn't mess with a fellow aviator's woman. Not if you had any respect for yourself or the uniform you wore.

Then again, warriors had been conducting raids and stealing women since time immemorial. The primal instincts Joe worked so hard to keep harnessed said Sue Ellen's sky jockey could damned well fight for his woman if he wanted to keep her.

As he looked down into that woman's highly indignant face, instinct won out.

"What the hell."

When he whipped his arm around her waist and hauled her against him, her jaw dropped again. Joe took instant advantage of her astonishment to cover her mouth with his.

The kiss was long and hard and left him greedy for more. Somehow, he managed to limit himself to just one taste.

When he set her on her feet, her look of mingled surprise and confusion afforded him almost as much satisfaction as that intensely erotic kiss. Not many men, he'd bet, caught Ms. Sue Ellen Carson off guard.

"What," she ground out, her eyes narrowed to slits, "was that?"

"Just a little souvenir to take home from camp."

Figuring he'd better quit the field while he was still ahead, Joe drew a knuckle down the curve of her cheek and beat a tactical retreat.

"See you tomorrow."

CHAPTER 9

Omigod! You're so brown!"

Andi's nose wrinkled delicately as she enfolded her friend in a fierce hug.

"And so, uh, fragrant."

Laughing, Sue Ellen returned her hug. "That, honey chile, is Eau d'Off! And this…"

She gestured to the teen who'd hung back during the parking lot reunion between parents, spouses and kids.

"…is Rose."

Andi had already cataloged the girl's ripe curves, jet-black hair and skin tinted to deep bronze after her weeks in camp. As Rose approached, she added dark, wary eyes to the inventory.

"Hi, Rose." Smiling, she extended a hand. "I'm Andi. Thanks for agreeing to help me out at the bookstore this summer."

"You're welcome. If you really need help, that is."

Andi had spent twenty-one years in uniform. Five of

those she'd served as a commander. She'd learned how to deal with just about every personality type, from nervous new recruits to crusty veterans with racks of combat ribbons on their chest.

Her people skills had been a significant factor in her recent election as mayor of Gulf Springs. They came into play now as she responded to Rose's question.

"The tourist trade has really picked up out on the island," she said easily. "Karen, my assistant manager, and I have been swamped."

The girl still looked doubtful, but Sue Ellen didn't give her time to debate the matter.

"Throw your gear in the back so we can say our goodbyes and get this show on the road."

Rose's backpack joined Sue Ellen's in the cargo well. Andi waited patiently beside the SUV while her two passengers exchanged hugs with an assortment of equally grubby men, women and teens. Rose, Andi noted, had to force the physical contact, but it came naturally to outgoing, gregarious Sue Ellen.

Except with Joe Goodwin.

Andi's brow hooked as she observed the brief interaction between S.E. and the chief. She couldn't hear their words, but their body language conveyed very interesting—and very mixed—signals. No hugs given or received, but the air around them seemed to crackle with some kind of suppressed electricity.

"What's with you and the chief?" Andi asked when Sue Ellen rejoined her.

"I'll tell you about it later. Right now, we'd better hustle. I borrowed Joe's phone and told Rose's foster mom we'd get to her place around ten."

TWENTY MINUTES LATER, Andi pulled up at the ranch-style house that had been Rose's home for the past five months. Like its neighbors, the cinder-block one-story was painted a cool pastel and sported a postage-stamp-size front yard showing more sand than grass. Bicycles and toys spilled off the front stoop and littered the yard. A dilapidated swing set sprouted like an overgrown weed in the back.

The scene suggested a home occupied by a large, happy family. The little Rose would share about the Scotts had painted a different picture. According to her, Harvey Scott was a regular at the greyhound track in Pensacola. His wife earned most of the family's income by caring for foster children in addition to her own.

Sue Ellen had been careful to avoid the issue of child-welfare payments during her phone call to the Scotts. She'd centered the conversation instead on the job at the book-store and used the requirement for Rose to complete STEP as a rationale for her spending the remainder of the summer with Sue Ellen. Since a judge had mandated Rose's participation in the STEP program, the Scotts were only too happy to let her "sponsor" assume full responsibility for getting her through it.

"That's Joan," Rose muttered, nodding to the thin, bottle-blonde unloading kids from a minivan.

"Andi and I will introduce ourselves while you pack your things." Sue Ellen twisted around in her seat. "Sure you don't want us to go in with you?"

Rose swept a glance up and down the block. Whatever she saw—or didn't see—seemed to reassure her. "I'm okay."

"We'll be right outside. Just yell if you need help carrying stuff out to the car."

The youngsters emerging from the minivan emitted whoops of joy when they spotted the newcomers. Like an unleashed pack, they charged across the yard.

"Rose!"

"You're home!"

"We missed you, W'ose."

That came from a toddler wearing pink flip-flops, a faded Princess Daisy T-shirt and a disposable diaper. Swinging the girl up, Rose planted a sloppy kiss on her cheek.

"I missed you, too."

"What did you bwring me?"

"A really neat rock. I found it in the river. It's shiny and pretty, just like your eyes, Bethie. And I've got a compass for you, Nick."

"Cool!"

"Com'on, guys." Hitching the toddler onto her hip, Rose herded the others toward the door. "I'll give you your presents inside. Then you can help me pack my stuff. I'm going to stay with…with my friend here for a few weeks."

The youngsters greeted the announcement with an instant chorus of protests.

"I've got a summer job," Rose said above the wails. "Tell you what! I'll use my first paycheck to take you all to Chuck E. Cheese."

The kids' obvious and very vocal affection provided Sue Ellen a different insight into Rose Gutierrez. With them, the girl shed her sullen mask and gave a glimpse of the real person beneath.

The mask snapped back into place, however, when Rose reappeared dragging a fat duffel and spotted the rusted clunker that rolled into the driveway behind the minivan.

It was as if someone had yanked down a window shade, Sue Ellen thought with a touch of dismay. Turning, she studied the kid who shouldered open the driver's door.

Someone should have told him that Grunge was *so*

nineties. His spiked hair and chain necklace made him look more wannabe nerd than hip. The acne-pitted moonscape of his face didn't add much to his image, either. He wasn't all that tall, maybe five-four or five, but developed enough to sport some serious muscle under his sleeveless black Nirvana T-shirt.

"This is our son, Brady," Joan Scott said by way of introduction. "Rose's foster brother."

"Where's she going?" the kid asked his mother, ignoring the visitors. "Hey! Where you going, Rosa-reeta?"

"None of your business, Pus Face. 'Bye, Joan. Let's go, Sue Ellen."

Silence reigned inside the Tahoe until the Scott house dropped out of the rearview mirror. Only then did Rose give an almost inaudible sigh and slide down in her seat.

Sue Ellen caught the sigh but didn't say anything until their volunteer chauffeur delivered them to the bayside condo. Andi helped the other two unload their gear and raised a questioning eyebrow.

"You still up for our appointments at the Golden Palm this afternoon, or would you rather use the time to help Rose get settled?"

"Are you kidding? You're looking at a face, hair and nails emergency. I'm good to go if Rose is?"

"Me?"

"Sure. I'll call first and twist Edward's arm so he'll squeeze us both in."

"Well…"

Sue Ellen took the hesitant reply as an assent and grabbed her backpack. "Let's get this stuff inside. The three of us will grab lunch, then head for the spa."

She felt like a stranger clumping into her cool, beautiful home in dusty boots and wrinkled cargo shorts. As if she'd been away far longer than three weeks and returned a different person, which she had, of course. In some ways.

It took her only a few moments to reacclimate, however. By the time she'd opened the plantation shutters and let light flood into the great room, she was home.

Rose followed the other two women, her thoughts churning. This was where Sue Ellen lived? Trying hard not to look stupid and google-eyed, she surveyed the marble floors, the high ceilings, the dramatic, rust-colored wall with its display of giant seashells. The inch-thick area rug in the great room almost tripped her and sent her crashing into a mirrored chest covered with gold curlicues. The piece looked like it had come out of some castle.

Jesus! She was supposed to live in this decorator's dream for several weeks? Plunk her butt into that fancy sofa with its fat, rolled arms?

"Hey, Ralph!"

Rose looked around to see Sue Ellen aiming for a plant set in an alcove flanked by tall columns.

"How're you hanging, pal? Pretty good, I see."

Stroking a glossy leaf, she caught Rose's eye.

"Say hello to Ralph the Rubber Tree. He's lived with me longer than either of my husbands."

What? Was she supposed to, like, *pet* the thing or something? Taken aback, Rose looked to Andi for guidance.

"I know," the tall, leggy brunette said with a laugh. "That would really sound pathetic unless you were acquainted with the two ex-husbands Sue Ellen refers to. Trust me, Ralph is a definite improvement."

Giving the plant a final pat, Sue Ellen continued the quick tour. "Com'on, Rose, I'll show you the kitchen before we take your stuff upstairs. Then I want to hit the shower. I've got three weeks of sand to scrub off."

The kitchen was as cool and elegant as the rest of the house. Rose slid a finger along the marble counter and tried not to gawk at the gleaming appliances.

"I stocked the fridge before I picked you up this morning," Andi told Sue Ellen. "How about I fix salad and sandwiches while you girls do your thing upstairs? I'll call Edward, too, and let him know he'll have three of us to exfoliate."

"Bless you, my child."

Rose kept her cool right up until she saw the TV in the guest room. The connecting bathroom with its lighted dressing table and oval tub sent her heart into a greedy, joyous leap.

"This bathroom is all mine?"

"Yep."

"Oh, man."

The soft sigh went straight to Sue Ellen's unabashedly sybaritic soul. She could imagine the pandemonium in the Scotts' house each morning, with a half dozen kids clamoring to use the bathroom. If nothing else, she could at least give Rose several weeks of long, uninterrupted bubble baths.

"We've got some time before we head to the spa. Want me to help you unpack?"

"I can manage."

"There are empty hangers in the closet. Here, let me help you lift that."

Bending at the knees, Sue Ellen grasped an end of the duffel and helped Rose set it on the bench at the foot of the bed.

"When we get home from the spa, we'll work out the logistics of getting you back and forth to the bookstore."

"Okay."

"You need to tell me what you like to do for fun, too, and a little about your friends. You're welcome to invite them over as long as I know about it in advance."

And was somewhere in the vicinity to supervise.

Sue Ellen had spent the past week mentally prepping to share her home with a teenager. She'd also received astute advice from her fellow Blues, along with several blunt warnings. The idea of rap booming through the built-in speakers, pizza cartons shoved under the bed and clothes scattered all over her serene, beautiful sanctuary made her throat go dry, but she'd just survived three weeks in the boonies. If she could ford rivers and wade through swamps, she could handle a few pizza cartons.

"I don't have any friends."

Rose's mutter jerked Sue Ellen from contemplation of the possible chaos to come.

"None?"

"I had to change schools when I moved in with the Scotts. It was the middle of the year and everybody was already hanging with their friends."

"What about your previous school? Anyone there you got close to?"

She knew she was forcing it, that Rose still wasn't ready or willing to open up. She'd backed off too many times before, though, to give up so easily.

"There was one guy…"

"Oh?" Encouraged by the grudging admission, Sue Ellen plopped onto the corner of the bed. "Tell me more. Is he cute?"

"Yeah, he is. Doesn't matter, though." Shrugging, Rose unzipped her duffel. "His dad is in the air force. They moved away."

"Oh."

She waited a few beats while her houseguest pulled midriff-skimming tops and jeans from her carryall.

"I'll tell you who I thought was definitely un-cute," she dropped casually. "Brady Scott wins the prize for butt-ugly."

Rose's mouth tightened. "Take it from me, he's as stupid as he is ugly."

"Is he the one who made those bruises on your neck?"

The girl flashed her a wary glance. "What bruises?"

"I saw them when we were on the way to camp."

When Rose didn't respond, Sue Ellen pressed the issue. "Did you tell your caseworker about them?"

"And what? Have her shuffle me off to another foster home? No, thanks. I can take care of myself."

"You shouldn't have to take care of yourself. There's a whole system that's supposed to do it for you."

"You don't have to tell me about the system. I know how it works. But I'm…"

She broke off, biting down on her lip.

"You're what?" Sue Ellen pressed. "It's okay. You can tell me."

"There's nothing to tell. Except…" Her jaw set, Rose tugged a sleep shirt out of the duffel. "The system has jerked me around for the last time."

"You're still a minor. You can't just take yourself out of the picture."

"Yes, I can! I turn seventeen in October. I can go wherever I want then. The police can't pick me up as a runaway. That's the law."

Five months, Sue Ellen thought with dismay. Five months until Rose dropped through the cracks. What would she do then? Join the ever-increasing ranks of young girls cruising the highways and truck stops?

Joe was so right to focus his program on teens her age. Rose and so many like her were only a half step away from being lost forever.

"You know, running away from problems doesn't really solve anything. Once you start running, you never stop."

The teen swept a glance around the room, lingering for a moment on the sleigh bed with its mounds of pillows, before she turned a scornful face to Sue Ellen.

"Like you know about running?"

"You're talking to a woman who lives alone except

for a plant named Ralph." Pushing off the bed, she made for the door. "Think about it."

ANDI, BLESS HER, HAD A tall pitcher of fresh-brewed iced tea waiting when Sue Ellen reappeared in the kitchen, showered, shampooed and shaved-legged.

"I called Edward. He'll work all three of us in."

"Thank God!" She joined her friend at the marble-and-wrought-iron table tucked in the sunny breakfast nook. "My face hasn't been creamed in three weeks. I can feel my skin crack every time I smile."

Andi passed her a tall, frosted glass. "You didn't sneak a jar of body lotion into your backpack?"

"I did. Turns out gnats love Chanel No. 5 as much as I do."

"Uh-oh."

"'Uh-oh' doesn't begin to describe it."

Downing a long, cool gulp, Sue Ellen related her battle with the brown cloud.

"Joe didn't exactly wave a copy of his prescribed list in my face, but he *did* remind me it didn't include perfumed cream. Several times, as a matter of fact. The latest being at the pickup point this morning."

When he'd pointedly refrained from brushing his knuckle over her cheek again, as he had last night. He'd wanted to, though. The urge was there, in his eyes, and damned if Sue Ellen's skin hadn't tingled in anticipation.

"Mmmm." Andi stirred the ice in her tea with a long-handled spoon. "Is that what you and the chief were discussing so heatedly? Face cream?"

"Actually, we were discussing the kiss he laid on me last night."

"Oh, reeee-ally?"

"Yes, reeee-ally." Sue Ellen's lips pursed in exasperation. "The man didn't have any better explanation for it this morning than he did last night."

"And that was?"

"He wanted to give me a souvenir," she said dryly, "from camp."

"A souvenir, huh?" Smirking, Andi took a sip of tea. "Sounds like you didn't spend *all* your time learning to read a compass."

"That's just it. I did. Mostly. I don't know where that kiss came from."

Her friend gave a snort that almost shot tea from her nose.

"Gimme a break, Sue Ellen! You know damned well you've perfected the come-hither look. All you have to do is walk into a room and flash those big, melting purples and every man in the place wants to take you to bed."

"Except I didn't flash them at Joe Goodwin. Okay, maybe a little. You have to admit he's a prime specimen."

"You get no argument from me on that point." Andi lifted a finger to conduct the chorus. "After all, he's…"

"*Special tactics.*" Sue Ellen sang it with her. "For a while yet, anyway."

"Dave mentioned the Chief's retirement ceremony is the end of this month. That's coming up fast. Did he say what he's going to do in civilian life?"

"Refine and expand his STEP program. It took me all those days and nights in the boondocks to come around, but I see now the program has real potential for statewide application. Maybe nationwide."

Refilling their glasses, Sue Ellen shared her impressions of Phase One and the team-building that had constituted Phase Two. Andi absorbed the details and asked several astute questions. She saved the most difficult one until Sue Ellen had wrapped up her evaluation.

"Sounds like Joe made a convert of you."

"He did."

"It also sounds as though you've developed more than a casual interest in the man."

Sue Ellen bit her lip. She had a good idea what was coming next.

"So where does Crash factor into the altered equation?" Andi asked.

"I don't know. I've been trying to figure that out."

"Well, you better come up with an answer pretty quick. Crash has a surprise for you."

"He told me. Something to do with pandas. What's that all about?"

"He wouldn't say. But I suspect he'll spring it on you this evening, when he comes over to welcome you home."

"In that case, I'd better add a pedicure to the afternoon's agenda. The boy has this thing for my toes."

CHAPTER 10

Three and a half decadent hours at the Golden Isle restored Sue Ellen to her former self.

Her hair feathered around her face in shining, white-gold layers. Her tanned and exfoliated skin tingled. Passionate Peach tipped her finger- and toenails, and her diamond once again graced her belly button, winking merrily above the waistband of her gauzy turquoise palazzo pants.

Rose's transformation was more subtle but no less impressive. Edward had clucked over the girl's chewed-to-the-quick nails and unplucked brows, but sighed rapturously as he thrust his hands through her thick, blue-black mane. Summoning an army of assistants, he'd supervised the buffing, plucking, cleansing, conditioning and, lastly, layering. A hesitant Rose emerged from the spa, still wary, still not ready to open up, but minus the scowl. A small smile actually snuck out when Andi and Sue Ellen oohed and aahed over her new look.

After confirming that Sue Ellen would bring Rose by the

bookstore for an orientation the following afternoon, Andi dropped them off at the condo.

"Guess I'll go up and finish unpacking," Rose murmured, obviously feeling a little disconcerted.

"You're welcome to listen to my iPod while you do. In fact, keep it with you and use it while you're here. I'll show you how to download songs from the computer later."

After Rose stuck in the ear buds and hit the stairs, Sue Ellen booted up her laptop, groaning at the more than four hundred e-mails in her inbox.

She'd worked her way through the first hundred or so when the doorbell rang. She greeted the handsome hunk on her stoop with a wide smile and a joyous leap of hormones.

"Hi, Crash."

He was more direct. Backing her against the doorjamb, he welcomed her home in his own inimitable way. Sue Ellen's newly refreshed makeup and hair had taken severe hits by the time he finished.

"Lord, I missed you, Susie-Q."

"I missed you, too."

Maybe not as much as she'd expected to, but he'd been there, in her thoughts, whenever Rose and the other Blues hadn't crowded him out. Or Joe, she added with a twinge of guilt as Crash held her at arm's length and conducted a swift inventory.

"You look good for a woman who slept in a pup tent for the past three weeks. *Very* good."

Delight swiftly substituted for guilt. Amazing what a little adoration could do for a girl.

"Thanks. You're looking pretty yummy yourself."

Polo might have stitched that sea-green shirt expressly for Crash's superbly conditioned physique. The knit fabric stretched across wide shoulders and tapered in at the waist of his drawstring khaki shorts. Boat shoes and a sexy grin completed the delicious ensemble.

He kept her in the loose circle of his arm as they wandered inside. "Ready for that surprise I mentioned?"

"I don't know. Am I?"

She was prepared for just about anything except the airline tickets he produced from his back pocket.

"What is this?"

"First class up and back to D.C. next weekend. Tai Shao is making his first public appearance."

"Who?"

"The newest baby panda at the zoo. The zoo is throwing him a big coming-out party."

"And I care because…?"

"Not into pandettes, huh? Okay, if Tai Shao doesn't do it for you, how about joining me in the honeymoon suite at the Ritz?"

"What?"

For a startled moment, Sue Ellen thought he was asking her to marry him. Her mind scrambled frantically for an answer but hadn't had time to come up with one before he expanded on his surprise.

"Our squadron had a couple of near misses while you were off communing with nature. I got tapped to participate on a task force to reevaluate the rules of engagement for joint air force-navy helo ops. I have to hop a plane to D.C., which…"

He cupped a hand around her nape and drew close again.

"…doesn't give me nearly enough time to welcome you home the way I'd planned to. I figured we could continue next weekend, in Washington. We'll do it in style, at the Crystal City Ritz-Carlton."

So much for a marriage proposal. Chagrined and more than a little relieved, Sue Ellen laid her palms on the sea-green knit and shook her head.

"Oh, Bill. I can't. I just got home and I—"

"Need to play some serious catch-up at work. I understand. But I'll be out of your hair all this coming week. You'll have five long, empty nights to fill with nothing but paperwork. I know you, Sue Ellen. You'll be ready to play come next weekend."

Ordinarily, she would. Despite the long hours she put in

during the week, she'd always made maximum use of her days off to indulge her vices...which most definitely included Major Bill Steadman.

"You're right, I will be ready to play. I just can't do it in Washington. I have someone staying with me for a while. She's upstairs now, getting unpacked. It's Rose," she explained in answer to his unspoken question. "The girl I'm sponsoring through STEP."

"You brought her home with you?"

"Until we work out other arrangements. Can you get your money back on the ticket?"

Taking his disappointment like a man, Crash stuffed the folder back in his pocket and reached for her. "If not, they'll apply it toward future travel."

His hands glided down her back and cupped her rear. Drawing her closer, he nestled her against his hips.

The familiar sizzle warmed Sue Ellen's veins. This she knew. This she could anticipate and enjoy with unabashed, hedonistic pleasure. The heat didn't jolt through her, as it had when Joe jerked her into his arms last night. But he'd surprised her. Caught her off guard. With Crash, the pace and intensity were hers to set.

"Wish you'd mentioned your houseguest when we talked the other night," he said, his voice dropping to a husky murmur. "I drove over here this afternoon all prepared to test your newfound survival skills."

The sizzle shot off delicious little sparks. Sue Ellen leaned into the bulge behind his zipper and slid her palms over the contours of his chest.

"I would have told you about Rose's visit, except I hadn't worked out all the arrangements yet and wasn't sure it would happen. I'm really sorry, Bill."

Not as sorry as she was a few minutes later, when the thump of footsteps on the stairs telegraphed an alert.

Peeling herself off Crash's chest, Sue Ellen raked hasty fingers through her disordered hair. She'd put herself more or less back together by the time her houseguest stopped on the threshold of the great room.

"Hey, Rose. This is my friend, Major Bill Steadman."

When Crash turned to greet her, the girl's eyes went as wide and round as computer disks.

Sue Ellen could sympathize with her goggle-eyed amazement. Major Steadman had had the same effect on *her* the first dozen or so times he'd aimed his killer smile her way.

"His buddies all call him Crash," she informed Rose, "but don't ask why. He won't go into specifics."

"Except to say my wild, hot-dawgging days are behind me. You can fly with me now in perfect safety and comfort."

"I don't *think* so!"

Rose's involuntary exclamation made Crash blink and Ellen burst into laughter.

"She's got you pegged, sweetie pie." Still chuckling, she swept an arm in a dramatic arc that included Rose. "You're looking at two beauties who spent the entire afternoon getting waxed and waved. Why don't you take us to dinner and show us off?"

CRASH NOT ONLY TREATED them to fat, juicy filets at the new steakhouse on U.S. 98, he engaged both women in a computerized game on Sue Ellen's laptop afterward.

Intergalactic Droid Zone was a cross between *Star Wars* and Pictionary. The game came with such brilliant graphics and dizzying special effects that Sue Ellen couldn't click the mouse fast enough when it was her turn to pin labels on the weird-shaped objects whizzing by. Defeated in the first round, she retired to the sofa and curled her legs under her while the other two sat on the Karastan with the laptop propped between them and duked it out.

"All right, Miss Smarty-Pants."

Dragging the pointer across the screen, Crash clicked on a distant star. A glowing pink centipede suddenly burst onto the screen. Mouth wide and voracious, the creature gobbled up the universe in greedy bites.

"Name that!" Crash hooted gleefully. "Ten seconds. Nine, eight, seven…"

"Ha! He's so last year."

Rose dug her shoulder into his and worked the track pad with a flying thumb and forefinger. Whatever answer she chose must have been correct, as the screen lit up like a neon Milky Way and one of Crash's spaceships exploded. Snickering, Rose flashed him a triumphant grin.

"You're totally dead."

"Not yet."

Eyes narrowed behind his ridiculously long lashes, Crash hunched next to Rose as she toyed with the track pad and searched for an object to sling at him.

Watching them, Sue Ellen experienced the weirdest sensation. For a second or two she felt uncomfortably like an indulgent parent watching two children at play. The startled realization made her squirm on the plush sofa.

Good Lord! Crash had never roused anything remotely resembling motherly feelings in her before.

Thoroughly disconcerted, it took her a moment or two to realize he was rousing a few sensations in Rose, as well. The sixteen-year-old was still wedged against him. She'd hunched her shoulders—deliberately or otherwise—and deepened the V of her neckline to expose the swell of her breasts. The glances she slanted Crash held a challenge that grew less playful and more provocative by the second.

Much like the glances Rose had aimed at Rafe Smith. She was ripe and ready, Sue Ellen thought with a jolt of another emotion altogether.

It wasn't jealousy. God knew, she'd *never* want to go back to Rose's age. She'd gone through all the wild highs and the crushing lows that come with the teen years. In the process, she'd fallen for her share of studs and had her heart dinged more than once.

What she had now was so much better. A great job and a busy life. A wide circle of friends. Glorious, steamy sex when she wanted it. No way she'd exchange the financial and emotional independence she'd worked so hard to achieve for the hormone rush of youth.

Still, it was probably just as well that Crash had to hop a plane to D.C. tomorrow. Her precarious relationship with Rose would unravel fast if the girl decided to compete for the chopper pilot's attentions.

THAT ROSE WANTED TO DO just that became clear after Crash departed around ten-thirty.

Sue Ellen walked him to his car, welcoming the warm night that wrapped around her with the same readiness she welcomed his arms.

"How long will you be gone?"

"I'm not sure."

Her lips pursed in a pout. "I go, you stay. I come home, you go. We need to work on our timing, fella."

"We need to work on more than that. You wouldn't consider slipping away for an hour or two?"

"I've been considering it since you drove up. Trust me, if this wasn't Rose's first night, you'd be wearing nothing but a satisfied smile right now."

Groaning, he bent and dropped a hard kiss on her lips. "I'm outta here, woman, before I spread-eagle you on the hood of my car and have my way with you."

Her pulse leapt, and she was seriously reconsidering her obligations to Rose when Crash disengaged.

"Go inside and play nice with the kid. I'll see you when I get back."

Sue Ellen's lips were still tingling from his kiss when she went inside. Rose had claimed the rolled-arm chair and was watching a horror flick on TV. Some fear-crazed teen crashed through a darkened house, shrieking at the top of her lungs. When her metal-fanged attacker burst from behind a door, Sue Ellen let out a small screech herself and hastily averted her eyes.

"Want some of Ben & Jerry's best?" she asked over the blood-curdling screams.

"Sure."

"Chunky Monkey or low-fat Cherry Garcia?"

Rose didn't take her eyes off the screen. "Whatever."

Thankfully, both the screams and the attacker had died by the time Sue Ellen returned with two heaping bowls.

"Here you go."

Rose tucked her legs under her and dug in. Sue Ellen plopped onto the sofa and did the same. The question she'd been anticipating came two mouthfuls later.

"So, are you and Crash doing it?"

Not tonight. Unfortunately.

"Off and on."

Rose's brow hitched. Her dark eyes met Sue Ellen's over a heaping spoonful.

"If he's as hot as he looks, why only off and on? Or is that none of my business?" she added when she didn't get an immediate response.

"No, it's okay."

First Andi, Sue Ellen thought wryly, now Rose. For the second time that day she struggled to define her relationship with Bill Steadman.

"We're friends, and lovers."

That summed it up pretty well, she decided…until Rose took a slow, catlike swipe at her spoon.

"But not *in* love, huh?"

They were getting a bit too personal here. Sue Ellen didn't want to feed the girl a line of bull, however, or cut off their first open exchange.

"I've been burned twice. I'm not in the market for another ex-husband. A lover who's also a friend is enough for me."

Rose took another slow lick. "I guess I can see that," she said after a moment. "And at your age, that's probably as good as it gets."

"Ouch!"

The exclamation brought color surging into the teen's cheeks. A second later the leaden mask dropped over her face with an almost audible clunk.

"Hey, you said it yourself. All you need is the occasional hump."

Sue Ellen hid another wince. Her relationship with Crash had sounded so much better when she'd framed it in her mind a few moments ago.

"I'm kinda tired. Mind if I go upstairs?"

"Not at all, but you don't have to ask my permission." Sue Ellen indicated the stoneware bowl with a casual tilt of her chin. "And you don't need to wash that. Just rinse it out and stick it in the dishwasher."

Rose arched a brow. "I was going to."

THE TEENAGER DIDN'T APPEAR for breakfast the next morning. Since it was Sunday and Andi's bookstore didn't open until noon, Sue Ellen let her sleep in and used the time to finish reading her e-mails.

There were several from her administrative assistant, most dealing with the schedule for the coming week. Every hour was crammed, Sue Ellen saw, but Alicia had managed to squeeze in the requested appointments with her attorney and Rose's caseworker.

The faint drone of the TV emanated from the guest room a little past 10:00 a.m. Rose appeared shortly after that, wearing jeans and a shirred, sleeveless blouse in a tawny-gold that gave her skin a warm glow.

After a late brunch, Sue Ellen put the top down on her sporty, midnight-blue Mustang convertible for the fifteen-mile drive to Andi's bookstore. It was located in the village of Gulf Breeze, on the western tip of Santa Rosa Island. Tourists who'd previously jammed into the Fort Walton Beach and Destin areas had begun to discover Gulf Breeze's relatively uncrowded sparkling white beaches. As a result, A Great Read did a brisk business in the latest whodunits and steamy romances, as well as books of local interest.

While Andi showed Rose around the bright-and-airy shop, Sue Ellen arranged with Karen Duchek, Andi's assistant manager, to pick up Rose on Monday, Wednesday and Friday mornings. The ginger-haired air force spouse lived only a few miles from Sue Ellen's condo and pooh-poohed her offer to pay for the gas.

"It's right on my way. Sorry I can't pick her up on Tuesdays and Thursdays. My boys have computer camp. They're enrolled in the summer program at the youth center on base the other days. Thank God!"

When Andi and Rose rejoined the two women, they worked out arrangements for the other two mornings.

"I'll pick you up on Tuesdays," Andi assured Rose. "I usually breakfast with the Gulf Springs City Council on Thursdays. I'll see if Dave or one of my other part-timers can swing by. As for driving you home in the evening, our schedules all vary but we'll work something out."

"Evenings aren't a problem," Sue Ellen said firmly. "I'll pick her up after work."

"You sure you can manage that?" Andi asked doubtfully. "We have our own version of rush hour since the Emerald Tower condos went on the market. You'll need to leave the office by five to beat the traffic coming across the bridge."

"Like I said, not a problem."

Not *much* of one, anyway. She'd have to force herself to shut down operations hours earlier than her usual 6:00 or

7:00 p.m. Alicia would probably keel over in shock when she heard of the arrangement. Resolutely, Sue Ellen stifled the wish she could detour by the office this afternoon and get a head start on the mounds of paperwork she knew would be waiting for her.

Meanwhile, Andi was giving Rose an outline of her duties.

"Here's the plan. We'll start you off in the back room unpacking boxes and scanning the contents into our computerized inventory system. When you feel comfortable with the system and layout of the store, you can stock shelves and assist customers. Karen or I will show you how to work the cash register when you're ready to start ringing up sales. How does that sound?"

Was she kidding? Rose thought incredulously.

It sounded like someone had just offered her a paid, summer-long vacation. With no scuffling kids to separate or loads of dirty clothes to shove into an ancient Kenmore or mattresses to scrub and disinfect after Bethie overflowed her diapers.

And no pimple-faced asshole sneaking into her room and trying to grope her, she thought with a surge of fierce satisfaction.

"Sounds okay."

A sudden doubt hit her as she raked a glance over Andi's

sleek white slacks and Karen's billowing, flower-print dress. Good God! Who wore lace-trimmed ankle socks and Mary Janes in summer?

"All I brought with me are jeans and T-shirts. And this blouse."

Andi put her doubts to rest. "Jeans and T-shirts are fine, as long as the message on the tee isn't too graphic or violent. If you'd feel more comfortable in something else, though, I'd be happy to give you an advance on your salary. You and Sue Ellen could hit the mall on your way home."

Rose bit back the "yes!" that sprang to her lips. She hadn't hung out at the mall in months, but she'd promised her first paycheck to Bethie and Chuck E. Cheese.

"I'm okay."

"If you change your mind, just let me know. So, it's all set, then. We'll see you tomorrow morning."

Hell, no, it wasn't set. Not in Rose's mind. She couldn't shake the bizarre feeling that aliens had abducted her and dropped her onto another planet.

These aliens were busy, successful women. They had men who loved them. Jobs they obviously enjoyed. Hot wheels. Expensive clothes.

Rose hadn't bought into the line Chief Goodwin and the other instructors had tried to feed the STEP participants. It was the same line her teachers and caseworker preached.

She'd heard that crap about hard work and education and teamwork being the keys to success so often she wanted to puke.

But looking at these women, seeing what they had, listening to what they offered her, started an itch inside Rose she ached to scratch.

"Yeah," she mumbled. "See you tomorrow."

The itch became almost unbearable when she accompanied Sue Ellen out of the shop. One day, she swore as her hungry gaze raked the Mustang parked at the curb, she'd own wheels like this.

"You have your driver's license, don't you?"

The casual question jerked her head around. The realization that she must have let her feelings show mortified Rose. Hadn't she learned the hard way to hide her thoughts, keep everything to herself? Letting someone inside your head made you too easy a target.

"I'm legal," she said gruffly.

Keys in hand, Sue Ellen leaned a hip against the driver's door. "How good are your driving skills?"

Good enough for a near escape in the neighbor's Dodge, Rose thought with a twist of her lips. She'd be in California now if Pus-face hadn't snuck into her room, discovered her empty bed and alerted his parents. The cops had stopped her at the on-ramp to I-10.

Still frustrated over the aborted attempt that had landed her in court and enrolled in STEP, Rose shrugged. "Joan had me run all her errands in the minivan. I usually took the kids with me, so I guess she thinks I'm an okay driver."

"Here you go, then."

The car keys arced through the air. Rose caught them in a tight fist and fought to keep the sudden spear of excitement from her voice.

"You want me to drive?"

"Yep."

Swallowing a huge mental gulp, Sue Ellen sauntered around to the passenger side. She knew she was taking a helluva risk here. Rose was still on probation for "borrowing" one car without the owner's consent.

"We'll see how the Mustang handles for you," she said, settling into the right-front seat. "Maybe once we get our schedules synced, you can take *me* to work in the morning and drive yourself back and forth to the bookstore."

Her mouth twisting, Rose slid behind the wheel. "Once you trust me not to go joyriding in your Mustang, you mean."

"You know the saying. Trust is a two-way street."

Sue Ellen had to grin at the rude noise that poofed out of Rose's lips.

"I know. That sounds trite as hell, but it's true. Let's just take it a week at a time," she suggested. "This week, you get chauffeured to work. Next week, we'll reassess the situation. Deal?"

Shoving the key in the ignition, Rose brought the powerful engine roaring to life.

"Deal!"

Sue Ellen braced herself for a knuckle-cracking return trip, but the teenager proved to be a very good driver. She kept a safe distance behind the car ahead and used her directional signals for lane changes. Her foot didn't get too heavy, either. Sue Ellen sincerely hoped it wasn't due to the fact that she was keeping a close eye on the speedometer. Still, she was having second and third thoughts about turning the Mustang over for other than quick hops to the grocery store or short mall trips.

"There's an electronics shop not far from the condo. We'd better stop and get you one of those cheapie, disposable cell phones." She masked her doubts behind a breezy smile. "With two schedules to coordinate, we'll need to able to communicate."

CHAPTER 11

A salty, seaweedy tang flavored the predawn air as Sue Ellen navigated the Pensacola Bay Bridge on her way to the office Monday morning. Her jumbo travel mug of coffee pumped juice into her system, but anticipation of reentering her own milieu provided the real rush.

She loved her job, very much enjoyed being the boss, and derived immense satisfaction from knowing she was damned good at what she did. After three weeks of bumbling through survival training, she had a spring in her walk as she slung her purse over her shoulder and covered the short distance from her reserved parking spot to the high-rise that housed her office.

Security at buildings occupied by federal agencies had tightened considerably since the Oklahoma City bombing and 9/11, but the guard on duty knew Sue Ellen well enough that she didn't have to flash her ID.

"Morning, Ms. Carson. You're in early."

"I have three weeks' work to catch up on."

"Looks like you had a great vacation," he commented. "You brought home a great tan."

"Yes, I did."

Along with calluses from her boots and pores permanently clogged with bug spray, but she didn't want to waste her precious quiet time explaining where she'd been the past three weeks. Spike heels clicking a sharp tattoo on the lobby tiles, she made for the elevator.

Her darkened office greeted her like an old friend. She had a good two hours before her staff arrived, three and a half before the first of her round of meetings. More than enough time to make a serious dent in the stacks of files Alicia had arranged neatly on her desk.

Shedding the short, bolero-style suit jacket she'd teamed with a slim skirt in the same pearl gray, Sue Ellen got the coffeepot going and settled in behind her desk. She whizzed through an application from a local marine engines remanufacturing firm to participate in the Federal Apprenticeship Program and approved the grant of ninety thousand dollars for the new technologies employment outreach program she'd reviewed prior to her incarceration at camp.

Next she tackled the multimillion dollar budget for the upcoming fiscal year her staff had put together. They'd agonized for months over anticipated funding cuts in several critical areas and adjusted accordingly. Sue Ellen's intense, line-by-line scrutiny ate up most of her quiet time, but she finished the review and dictated her comments into the microphone built into her desk computer just as the sun gilded the glass-fronted high-rises along the waterfront.

The next folder in the stack generated a wry smile. She opened the manila folder and there was her disapproval of federal funding for Chief Goodwin's STEP program, staring her right in the face.

"Okay, Joe. You've got your grant."

Reactivating the mike, she dictated a letter authorizing the funds she'd earmarked for STEP in the budget she'd just reviewed. Ordinarily, her director of Disadvantaged Youth Employment Programs would monitor the program from that point, but Sue Ellen saw no point in duplicating efforts.

"Memo to Howard Trask."

She spoke directly into the mike, giving thanks for the voice-recognition technology that would translate her spoken words into the proper format, assign a time and date, and whiz the memo to the appropriate staff member.

"Since I survived… Strike that. Begin memo again. Since I completed Phases One and Two of STEP and am sponsoring a participant through the follow-on phases, I have a good grasp of the program's goals. I'll review the quarterly STEP metrics and provide the necessary input for our required reports."

The quarterly metrics review involved a face-to-face with the program coordinator, aka Joe Goodwin, but that hadn't driven Sue Ellen's decision. As Rose's sponsor, she'd meet with Joe Goodwin at least once a month, anyway. Which reminded her…

"Memo to Alicia. Please schedule a meeting with Chief Goodwin within the next thirty days. No, make that within the next two weeks."

Joe would want to know the results of Sue Ellen's session with Rose's caseworker.

"Oh, and I expect a call from a Mr. Roger Bendix. He's coordinating a meeting for my team from camp. Do whatever is necessary to make that happen."

Funny how her life had become so intertwined with STEP. She and Joe Goodwin would be seeing a lot of each other in the coming weeks. Just as well. That would give Sue Ellen time to assess where the heck the man had been coming from with his kiss…and where she wanted him to go. In between, she'd better figure out what to do about Bill Steadman.

She and Crash hadn't exchanged any vows. Nor had they specifically agreed *not* to see other people. Yet Sue Ellen operated under the old-fashioned and inconvenient premise that going to bed with a man, even on an occasional basis, carried its own set of obligations.

She felt a sneaky guilt that Crash was out of the picture

for a few weeks while Joe would pop up on her radar screen with some frequency. She had to work at it, but managed to rationalize away the guilt.

She'd be seeing Joe on business, probably with others in attendance. That alone would put the kabosh on any opportunity for physical contact…unless Sue Ellen engineered a more private setting. Best to see how their first meeting went, she decided as she picked up the unmistakable sounds of her administrative assistant's arrival.

She went to greet Alicia and got a warm welcome home. Ten minutes later, her day had kicked into superdrive.

DESPITE THE AVALANCHE OF phone calls to return, staff waiting to see her and planning sessions to attend, Alicia had carved time out of Sue Ellen's hectic schedule for the two personal meetings she'd requested.

The first was with her lawyer. Peter Chobanian occupied a suite of offices in Pensacola's Historic Village district. The five-block area boasted green parks and red brick buildings clustered around remnants of the fort that dated from the arrival of the Spanish in 1559, all fronting the bay.

"So," Peter said when she settled in the ox-blood leather wing chair in front of his desk. "Your ex isn't giving you grief about the termination of his alimony, is he?"

"Other than a few whining phone calls and e-mails, no."

"Good, good." He steepled his fingers under his heavy jowls and cranked up a grin. "I'm assuming you haven't come to discuss another divorce."

"Not hardly. You know I've sworn off husbands for the foreseeable future."

"What can I do for you, then?"

"This is probably out of your area, but I need to know the legalities involved in assuming temporary responsibility for a sixteen-year-old unrelated to me."

"How temporary?"

"I'm not sure. Several weeks. Perhaps as long as several months."

"Are you talking legal guardianship, as granted by a court or judge?"

"Right now it's an informal arrangement. I have her foster parents' verbal permission for her to stay at my place. And I'm meeting with her caseworker this afternoon to advise her of the arrangement. But, well..."

Peter's fleshy cheeks creased into a smile. "There's always a caveat in this business."

"Rose—the girl—has been picked up as a runaway several times. She also borrowed a neighbor's car for a joyride a few months back. If something happens while she's under my supervision, I want to know my responsibility in the matter. And my liability."

The issue of liability hadn't kept Sue Ellen awake at night, but she'd plucked Rose out of her court-mandated residence. If there were legal ramifications, she needed to be aware of them sooner rather than later.

"Very wise of you," her attorney concurred. "And you're right, this is out of my area of expertise. I'll call an associate who specializes in family law and see what she has to say."

"Thanks, Peter."

"Have you checked with your insurance company regarding third-party coverage for your home and auto?"

"I have. I'm covered."

"Good, good." He waited a beat, regarding her with heavy-lidded eyes. "There's something else?"

Sue Ellen hesitated. She wasn't sure about her next request. As far as she knew, the authorities hadn't been able to locate Rose's grandmother. Or if they had, the woman had either refused or was in no condition to care for a small child. Yet Sue Ellen could still hear the longing in Rose's voice when she'd talked about her grandmother's garden.

"Do you still use the services of that private investigator who got the goods on my late and unlamented ex?"

"I do."

"I'd like him to trace someone for me. I don't have a name or address or social security number."

"What *do* you have?"

"Rose Gutierrez's birthday and place of birth. He'll have to work backward from Rose's birth certificate to her mother's, and then to *her* mother's."

"That's who you want to locate? The maternal grandmother?"

"That's who I want."

SUE ELLEN'S AFTERNOON meeting with Rose's caseworker plunged her into the unfamiliar bureaucracy of Florida's Department of Children and Families. Somewhat to her surprise, she learned DCF had contracted with a private firm to manage the foster care program. FamiliesFirst occupied a modern building on Moreno Street, not far from Sue Ellen's office.

Rose's caseworker came out to greet her and escorted her back to a small conference room. A cheerful and obviously overworked woman who looked to be in her mid-fifties, Marta Perry produced an organizational wiring diagram that rivaled the U.S. Department of Labor's for complexity and layers.

"Your secretary indicated you were unfamiliar with our operation, so I thought I'd give you a quick overview. As DCF's primary sub-agent, we manage community-based care in conjunction with foster parents and the District One Community Alliance agencies you see here."

Sue Ellen struggled to follow the dotted lines for intake, home approval and placement. "FamiliesFirst approves couples who apply to become foster parents, right?"

"Right." The social worker flipped to another chart. "But only after each application is reviewed by a committee composed of these agencies."

"And you make the decision where to place children who are entered in the system?"

"We do, again subject to review by a committee that includes a court-appointed child welfare advocate and the primary DCF focal point for that case."

"How often do you make home visits to check on the children?"

"The law requires quarterly visits. I check on my kids at least once a month, in person if possible, by phone if not."

"Rose told me she's been in several foster homes over the years," Sue Ellen said slowly. She was skirting on dangerous ground here, but she couldn't get the memory of those bruises out of her mind. "Has she indicated any problems with her present family?"

Marta stuffed the organizational chart in her desk drawer before replying.

"I'm sorry, Ms. Carson. I know you're Rose's STEP sponsor, and you've told me she's staying with you while she works at a summer job you've arranged for her. I'm thrilled you're taking such an interest in her. God knows, it's time someone did. But I can't violate her privacy by discussing the specifics of her case with you or anyone else outside our system."

"I understand."

"I will say this, however."

The older woman angled her head and treated her visitor to a careful scrutiny. Sue Ellen got the distinct impression there wasn't much the caseworker hadn't seen or dealt with over the years.

"Florida law *requires* every person to report a suspected case of child abuse. So let me turn your question around. Has Rose indicated any problems to you regarding the family she's currently residing with?"

Sue Ellen had her suspicions, mostly involving the Scotts' pimply son, but she couldn't make such serious accusations without a shred of proof.

"Rose told me she doesn't want go back there," she replied, choosing her words carefully, "but she won't say why."

"I see." The caseworker's shoulders slumped for a moment. "I had so hoped…" She caught herself and forced a smile. "I'll speak with Rose as soon as possible."

"Just name the day and time. I'll drive her in."

"You've given me your home address and the address of

the bookshop where she's working," the woman replied in a tone of gentle rebuke. "I'll find her."

Belatedly Sue Ellen realized the social worker no doubt preferred to make unannounced visits. That was fine by her.

Having accomplished her goal of alerting the appropriate agency to Rose's present whereabouts and situation, she hitched her purse over her shoulder.

"Thanks for your time, Ms. Perry. As you say, I'm presently outside the system and there's only so much you can tell me. But I promised Rose I'd do whatever I could to help her. I want you to know I intend to follow through on that promise."

"Good!"

The social worker rose as well and took the hand Sue Ellen held out in a bone-crunching grip.

"You do that, and I'll do my job. Between us, we'll get Rose through this rough patch."

SUE-ELLEN'S SATISFACTION WITH THE results of both visits carried her through the rest of her cram-packed afternoon.

She left the office at five, much to Alicia's surprise and delight. Lugging a bulging briefcase, she joined the throng exiting the building and prepared to do battle with the bumper-to-bumper rush hour traffic.

Once across the Bay Bridge, Highway 98 opened up. The tall, spindly pines crowding either side of the road dappled the pavement. Sue Ellen whizzed through the patchwork of shadow and light, her mind darting from all she'd accomplished her first day back at work to all that yet needed doing. The wheels were still churning when she parked her Mustang outside A Great Read.

As she reached for the door latch, she spotted a broad back and familiar set of shoulders topped by a head with salt-and-pepper hair shaved close to the scalp. Joe Goodwin leaned against the front counter, chatting with Rose and Karen Duchek.

Telling herself she'd have to think about the pleasure that zinged through her veins, Sue Ellen pushed at the door. The tinkle of the bell mounted about the leaded-glass panel brought Joe's head around. His glance roamed over her, taking in the three-inch heels, the slim skirt, the saucy bolero jacket.

"You look a little different from the last time I saw you," he said with a smile.

"So do you."

He was in uniform. Not BDUs this time, but dark blue slacks and a light blue, open-necked shirt. His silver belt buckle glinted in the afternoon sunlight, as did the silver wings above his rack of colorful ribbons. The array of stripes on his shoulder tabs gave visible testimony to his rank and authority. The maroon beret tucked under his belt added its own cachet.

Tearing her gaze away, Sue Ellen greeted Karen and Rose. Curiosity pulled her attention back to Joe. That, and the pleasure still curling through her.

"Are you checking up on Rose and me already?"

"Nope. I came by to deliver these." He tapped a finger on a stack of square envelopes lying on the counter. "But as long as I was here, I thought I'd get an update. I was just asking Rose about her first day on the job."

Mentally crossing all twenty fingers and toes, Sue Ellen turned to the teen. "How did it go?"

"Okay."

"Just okay?"

The questions put Rose on the spot. Shoving her hands in the pockets of her jeans, she hitched her shoulders.

"Well, that wand thing is fun. I liked scanning in the books. Other than that, I just emptied boxes and flattened them."

"The rest will come, as Andi told you." A twinkle lit Karen's eyes. "You did a great job of flattening those cartons, by the way."

The girl's embarrassed expression said "big deal," but for once she didn't voice her thoughts.

Sue Ellen swallowed a relieved sigh. The first day on a new job was always tough. Rose seemed to have navigated the rocky shoals.

While she reveled in the moment, Joe shuffled through the envelopes and passed one to Rose. "This is for you. I brought one for you and your family, Karen. For Andi and Dave, too."

Sue Ellen was feeling left out until he produced another from his pocket.

"I was going to deliver this to your office personally, but since you're here…"

The envelope was thick vellum, with the air force seal embossed in silver on the flap. Rose already had hers open.

"Wow, this is cool."

And very impressive, Sue Ellen thought as she scanned the engraved lettering.

The Commander, 16th Special Operations Wing, requested the pleasure of her company at a parade and ceremony celebrating the retirement of Chief Master Sergeant Joseph Goodwin, 1500 hours, the thirty-first of May. Reception to follow.

The invitation included a phone number to RSVP, but all three women provided a direct response.

"Jerry and I and the boys will be there," Karen assured him.

"Me, too," Rose said, fingering the engraved lettering with some awe.

Joe turned to the petite blonde at his side. He'd wanted to deliver the invitation and get her answer in the relative privacy of her office. Too bad she'd nixed his move by showing up at the store.

"What about you, Ms. Sue Ellen?"

"I wouldn't miss it. Thanks for including me."

Joe didn't want her thanks. What he wanted was a repeat of that kiss Friday evening. So bad he hurt with it.

He'd carried the taste of those lush red lips in his head for three days now. He'd carried images of the rest of her, too, from her high, proud breasts to the hips that flared so enticingly below her dainty waist.

The Sue Ellen who'd occupied his thoughts the entire weekend generally wore boots and cargo shorts and wrinkled camp shirts. He suspected the one standing next to him would compete for space with that one inside his head for a good many nights to come. Did the woman have *any* idea how that short, saucy jacket made a man itch to slide his hands under the lapels and peel them back, inch by slow, exploratory inch?

Who was he kidding? Of course she did. Ms. Carson was well aware of her effect on the male of the species and used it to great advantage. Like with her pretty flyboy.

Joe hadn't consciously pumped Rose for information prior to Sue Ellen's arrival, but he had no trouble reading between the lines of what she'd told him. Apparently Sue Ellen had departed camp, spent hours getting gorgeous and fallen right into the arms of the major.

That would have seriously torqued his jaws if Rose hadn't also let drop that the chopper pilot had spent the evening of their homecoming playing video games with her instead of the kind of games he'd no doubt planned to play with Sue Ellen. And according to Rose, Steadman was now in Washington, where he indicated he might have to remain for an unspecified period of time.

His loss, Joe thought with a visceral satisfaction, and my gain. Ms. Carson didn't know it yet, but her days as a free agent were numbered.

He'd planned to make his move this week. Tonight, if all had gone as scripted with the invitations. The knowledge that Pretty Boy Steadman was out of the picture for a while altered Joe's approach.

Instinct and the hunter's skills he'd perfected over the past three decades told him to throttle back, let Sue Ellen wonder, wait for *her* to make the next move…even if the waiting put a permanent kink in his gut. He could feel it there, low in his belly, as he forced himself to change his angle of attack.

"I'm hosting a dinner for a few friends after the retirement ceremony. I'd like you to come."

Was that a flicker of satisfaction in her wide eyes? Or surprise at how slowly he was playing his hand? Joe was damned if he could tell.

"The invitation includes your troop, Karen and Rose as well. I'm hoping the Colonels Armstrong can make it, too."

"All my favorite people," Sue Ellen said with an easy smile. "Count me in."

"Great. Othello's," he told her. "At 6:00 p.m."

"Othello's. At 6:00 p.m. I'll be there."

CHAPTER 12

In the days preceding Chief Goodwin's retirement ceremony, Sue Ellen's tenuous relationship with Rose should have improved. Instead, it seemed to fray at the seams.

Her killer schedule at the office was certainly a contributing factor. The heavy responsibilities she'd always thrived on now required constant juggling so she could leave work in time to pick Rose up. As a result, she progressed from carrying home one briefcase to two and spent long hours going through the work in both each evening.

Rose didn't complain about her preoccupation. If anything, the teen considered it a reprieve from forced conversation. She spent *her* evenings glued to the TV or up in her room, sprawled across her bed with the earbuds of Sue Ellen's iPod stuffed in her ear canals. With Sue Ellen's permission, she'd downloaded her favorite songs from the Internet and made no effort to disguise the fact that she preferred Christina Aguilera's company to that of her sponsor.

Given Rose's preference for solitude, Sue Ellen certainly

couldn't complain that her houseguest was intrusive or disruptive. Nor did she display the sloppy habits Paul Sr. and Delilah said came naturally to teens. Rose made her bed every morning and was scrupulous about hanging up her clothes. She even sponged her shower after every use, something her hostess usually forgot to do.

So there wasn't any real reason for Sue Ellen to feel so…so crowded. Or so damned edgy.

The sneaky sensations kept creeping up on her, though, until she slammed down the lid on her laptop Thursday evening and made herself analyze them.

"What's with me?" she groused to the silent, always supportive Ralph. "Why am I feeling so snarky?"

His glossy leaves seemed to quiver in sympathy, but he offered no concrete advice or suggestions.

"I know where part of it is coming from," she informed the attentive rubber plant. "The initial flush of victory has passed. I kept my promise. I removed Rose from the Scotts, for the time being, anyway. I found her a summer job, got her caseworker's tacit approval for the arrangement. I even accompanied her to the Blues' first reunion and Phase Four planning session."

Which, Sue Ellen now realized with the benefit of twenty-twenty hindsight, had increased rather than decreased the responsibilities she'd so blithely assumed.

The Blues had jumped on Roger Bendix's suggestion that they focus their community involvement project around the copper mask recovered from the Blackwater River. It seemed like such a great idea when they'd discussed it.

They would research this area's Native American tribes. Work up a digital display of artifacts, centered on the mask the two Pauls had turned over to Northwest Florida University. Offer an interactive presentation to local groups like the Boy Scouts and garden clubs and senior citizen centers. The project would not only increase local residents' awareness of northwest Florida's rich cultural heritage, it would educate the Blues in the process.

All well and good, except Sue Ellen and Rose were now on the hook to produce a design for the digital display. So far neither of them had found either the time or inclination to kick around ideas. Sue Ellen's rash promise to have something by the Blues' next meeting this coming Saturday only added to the pressure she felt piling up on her.

"Then there's this business with Joe Goodwin," she muttered, pinching a brown tip from one of Ralph's leaves. "I can't figure the man out. I was sure he'd at least *try* to pick up where we left off at camp."

So sure, she'd convinced herself that he'd timed his visit to the bookstore Monday afternoon to intercept her. So sure, her toes had curled in delicious anticipation when she'd spotted him through the leaded glass. Yet all he'd done was issue a group invitation to everyone present.

Did he, or did he not, want to take this...this whatever it was...any further?

Did she?

"How the hell can I decide," she asked Ralph indignantly, "when we've never been alone more than two or three minutes at a stretch?"

Ralph had no answer.

And how pathetic was she, communicating her problems to a rubber plant! Irritated with herself, the world in general and Chief Goodwin in particular, she flipped open her laptop.

THE PHONE CALL SHE RECEIVED a half hour later added another layer to her frustration.

"It's Doyle Andrews, Ms. Carson. Sorry to bother you at home, but you said to call anytime I had an update."

She shot a quick glance over her shoulder to make sure Rose hadn't wandered downstairs. Sue Ellen hadn't told her about the P.I. she'd hired to search for her grandmother. She didn't want to raise false hopes, or slap the teen with another painful rejection if it turned out her grandmother hadn't wanted anything to do with her as a child and refused to acknowledge her now.

"No problem. What have you found?"

"Nothing, I'm afraid. I've hit a dead end."

Well, hell!

Sue Ellen had warned herself repeatedly not to nurse the secret fantasy that Rose's grandmother would magically resurface, weeping tears of joy and whisk her granddaughter out of the condo into a vine-covered cottage. Still, the P.I.'s report generated a sharp sting of disappointment.

"I thought you had a good lead on the Anna Maria Gutierrez listed on Rose's mother's birth certificate?"

"I thought I did, too."

From his previous report, Sue Ellen knew Andrews had found thirty-seven women by that name in Miami-Dade County, where Rose's mother had been born. She'd gulped at the number, but it turned out P.I.'s had access to sources not available to the general populace. By cross-referencing marriage, divorce, employment, education, financial and death records, he'd quickly winnowed down the list to three probables.

Two, Andrews had reported, were deceased. One, Sue Ellen now learned to her bitter disappointment, had disappeared off the face of the earth.

"I tracked her as far as Ybor City. It's a small, predominantly Hispanic community on the outskirts of Tampa."

"I know where it is."

The Department of Labor operated an outreach program in Tampa tailored specifically for the many Hispanics of Cuban descent living in the area. Florida's governor had recently recognized the program as one of the most innovative employment-growth opportunities in the state.

"Anna Maria Gutierrez moved to Ybor City five years after her husband's death. That was three years before her only daughter dropped out of school and hit the road."

Where she got pregnant, Sue Ellen thought grimly, gave birth to a daughter and hauled her baby from crack house to crack house until the mother OD'd and her four-year-old ended up a ward of the state.

"I found a deed recording the sale of a two-bedroom house to one Anna Marie Gutierrez," the P.I. reported. "She was still living at that address when Rose was born, but sold it in 1994."

Sue Ellen had to ask. "Did it have a garden?"

"Excuse me?"

"The house. Do you know if it had a rose garden?"

"The deed doesn't include that kind of information. I can try to get the records from the realty company that handled the sale, but I doubt they'll have kept the data all this time."

"I guess it doesn't matter if Anna Maria doesn't live there any longer."

"As I said, she sold the place in '94. That's when she

dropped out of sight. I've checked every database I can legally access and a few I'm not supposed to be able to get into. I can't find a record of anyone with her name and SSN after May of that year."

Sue Ellen milked a few drops of hope from the fact that he hadn't turned up Anna Maria's death certificate.

"Do you want me to keep working the search? I can't do it this week, but I could drive down to Tampa next week and talk to her neighbors. Someone might know what happened to her."

Tampa was only about a five-hour drive. At $500 a day plus expenses, he wouldn't run up too high a tab.

"Go ahead and make the trip. You've got my cell phone and work number. Please call me if you find anything."

"Will do."

THEIR CONVERSATION LINGERED in Sue Ellen's mind until she went upstairs an hour later.

Rose met her at the top of the stairs. She was in a faded cotton tee with a hem cut well above the waist of low-riding hipsters. The display of nubile young curves didn't particularly improve Sue Ellen's mood.

Rose's wasn't too great, either. She'd had to borrow a box of tampons earlier, which might have something to do with the hands now balled on her hip.

"You know I get my first paycheck this coming Tuesday."

"Yes, I do."

"I told you I want to use it to take Beth and the other kids for pizza."

"You did, but I thought we agreed that excursion had to wait until next weekend. I'm up to my ears all next week with…"

"You don't have to go with me. I've driven the Mustang to the grocery store a bunch of times now, and you let me cruise the beach after dinner last night. I can take the kids myself."

"They won't all fit in the Mustang. Not with car seats for Beth and the other one, the little boy. I told you I'd borrow Andi's Tahoe."

Sue Ellen headed for her bedroom. Rose dogged her heels.

"I've got Tuesday afternoon off," she said with stubborn persistence. "I want to take them then."

Sue Ellen's jaw tightened, but she kept her cool as she tugged at the drawstring bow on her gathered shorts. "I told you. I have an important meeting scheduled that afternoon. I can't cancel it."

"You don't have to. Andi will let me borrow the Tahoe if you ask her."

"I won't do that. As long as you're staying with me, my

insurance covers you driving *my* vehicle. I don't know what Andi's coverage is."

"So ask her. Never mind, I'll ask her myself."

"No, you won't. Dammit, Rose, don't walk away! I'm talking to you."

The slam of the guest room door tightened Sue Ellen's mouth. Seeing red, she stalked out of her bedroom and hammered a fist on the white-painted panel.

"Go away!"

"The hell I will. This is my house. Open the door and we'll finish our conversation."

"It's finished."

"No, it's not. Open up."

She'd made a solemn vow to respect Rose's privacy, but the urge to whap the damned door back on its hinges grew by the second. She managed to refrain, although her peach-tinted nails had gouged deep grooves by the time Rose yanked the door open.

Unfortunately, the heavy panel got away from her and did just what Sue Ellen had contemplated mere seconds ago. With a violent swing, the door slammed into the wall. The very expensive French porcelain handle made violent contact with the stucco. As flakes of plaster floated to the carpet, Sue Ellen's jaw went so tight she was sure her teeth would crack.

"Sorry."

The gruff apology was all that saved Rose from instant annihilation. That, and her offer to pay for the damage.

"If it's not enough to fix the hole in the wall, you can deduct the rest from next week's pay."

Sue Ellen was just pissed off enough to accept the offer. "I will," she snapped. "In the meantime, let's be sure we understand each other. I'm responsible for you, not Andi. I don't want you asking to borrow her car. It's enough she helped us both out by giving you a job."

"Okay. Fine. Anything else?"

"No. Good night."

"Good night."

GIVEN THE DISPARITY IN their work hours, Sue Ellen didn't have an opportunity to mend fences with Rose before departing for the office early Friday morning.

She made what she considered a noble effort by propping a note on the kitchen table, saying she was sorry for the sharp exchange last night and would see Rose at the bookstore at two that afternoon.

She'd arranged to meet her, Andi and her husband, Dave, at the shop and drive to nearby Hurlburt Air Force Base with them. Joe's retirement ceremony was scheduled for three, which *should* have given them plenty of time to make the short trip.

Naturally, the hour-long, eight-way video-conferencing call with the other Employment and Training Administration regional directors scheduled for noon ran until almost one-thirty. Then an accident on the Bay Bridge backed traffic up for miles.

Cursing under her breath, Sue Ellen apprised Andi by cell phone of her inch-by-inch progress and changed their rendezvous point from the bookstore to the parking lot of a 7-Eleven a half mile from Hurlburt's front gate. She screeched into the lot at two-forty, dashed to the Tahoe and scrambled into the back seat beside Rose.

"Sorry! I was about to call you and tell you to go on without me."

Andi slewed around as far as her seat belt would allow. "Glad you made it. Joe would have been disappointed if you'd missed the big event."

Ha! Sue Ellen wasn't so sure about that. The chief had managed to go four whole days now without a word, but who was counting?

His silence was in direct contrast to Crash, who'd called twice to tell Sue Ellen he hadn't canceled the plane tickets. Just in case she changed her mind about flying up to D.C. this weekend.

She was sorry now she'd said no.

The weekend looked to be a total bitch at this end. She *still* hadn't worked up a design for the meeting with the Blues tomorrow. And Rose was obviously *still* pissed about the pizza thing. She'd barely glanced at Sue Ellen before turning to stare out her window. The prospect of spending the weekend trying to coax her out of her mood was daunting, to say the least.

Blowing out a long breath, Sue Ellen used the short transport to the 16th Special Operations Wing headquarters to repair her makeup. There wasn't much she could do for her lime-green linen suit. The suit showed the effects of hours at the office, but hopefully the eye-popping jungle-green-and-pink silk blouse she'd paired it with would draw attention away from the wrinkles.

She had herself more or less together again by the time Dave turned into the parking lot alongside a monstrous aircraft hangar. Since Dave had formerly commanded one of the wing's key combat elements, he was instantly recognized and waved to VIP parking.

Five minutes later, they had programs in hand and were headed for the crowd seated in folding chairs lined up inside the hangar.

"Rose! Sue Ellen!" Brenda's shiny gold curls popped above the crowd. "We saved you seats!"

Waving enthusiastically, the teenager beckoned them

over. The rest of the Blues were there, Sue Ellen saw, along with a good number of Yellows and Reds.

"Go ahead," Andi said when she hesitated. "Dave and I will sit with Karen, Jerry and the boys."

Once Sue Ellen and Rose had joined their teammates, Brenda fell into renewed raptures over Rose's more subtle makeup and layered hairdo.

"Wow! You look *hot!* You should wear your hair framing your face like that all the time." She dug an elbow into the kid seated next to her. "Shouldn't she?"

"Looks good to me," Jackson agreed as he, in turn, elbowed his brother. "Move your buns, Ev. Rose is gonna sit here."

Hooking a finger to loosen the tie encircling his bulldog neck, the elder McPhee shifted and added his approval of Rose's new look before running an approving eye over Sue Ellen.

"I'd say we all clean up pretty good."

She couldn't argue with that. In camp, the Blues had worn a motley array of shorts, jeans and wrinkled shirts. When they'd held their initial Phase Four planning session, they upgraded to normal work and play clothes. Today they were decked out in their Sunday best.

Paul Sr. and Paul Jr. looked hot but spiffy in suits, white shirts and ties. Roger Bendix had dressed for the occasion by inserting a small American flag in the lapel of his tweedy jacket. Dylan's shaggy brown hair flowed over his collar, making him a standout among the military males with their white sidewalls, but he was otherwise very presentable.

"Where is the Black team sitting?" Rose asked.

"They're not sitting," Dylan told her, pointing to the phalanxes of uniformed personnel across the hangar. "They're standing. See, there's Singer and Jordan. And Rafe Smith."

"Where?"

"There, in the second rank or squad or whatever they call it."

Rose craned her neck and searched the massed formations. They were backed by an array of firepower that included a C-130 Hercules bristling with armament, a Pave Hawk helicopter and several aircraft Sue Ellen couldn't put a name to. She suspected Joe had flown in, rappelled from or jumped out of every one of them in his long career.

"I see Singer and Jordan," Rose said with a frown, "but not Rafe."

"He's right there, at the end of the second row."

"Oh, okay. I've got him now."

Just moments later a drum roll was followed by a booming command. "A-tennnnnn-*shun!*"

With a thunderous clap of boot heel hitting boot heel, the air commandos massed across the hangar whipped to attention.

"Ladies and gentlemen, please stand for the arrival of the reviewing party."

The crowd surged to their feet, and the band broke into a lively march. Joe marched in shoulder-to-shoulder with the commander of the 16th Special Operations Wing. He and the colonel stayed in lockstep, their heels drumming a tattoo on the shiny, painted floor. As one, they clicked to a halt at right angles to the color guard.

One polished boot went behind the other. Shoulders square, chin high, Joe and the colonel executed a right face so precise and razor sharp they might have been welded together.

"Preeeeeeeee-sent, h-*arms!*"

Hundreds of uniformed arms snapped up in perfect unison. The 16th Special Operations Wing flag dipped. So did the air force flag with its mass of colorful streamers. The American flag stood tall.

With a swell of emotion, Sue Ellen put her hand over her heart and joined in the singing of the national anthem.

Halfway through the last refrain, her gaze dropped from the Stars and Stripes to the man standing with his arm at a rigid forty-five-degree angle, his hand knife-blade straight and just touching his brow.

Oh, Joe! I hope to God you find something to replace all you're saying goodbye to here.

CHAPTER 13

The reception following the retirement ceremony was lavish, lively and spiked with laughter. Joe's troops presented him with a host of farewell gifts that ranged from a pearl-handled commemorative Special Operations pistol to a leather recliner to facilitate his transition to his new couch-potato lifestyle.

Joe made the rounds and spoke to each of the several hundred guests but lingered for some time with Sue Ellen, Andi, Dave and Rose. After congratulating the chief and giving him a shy hug, Rose wandered off in search of punch, or so she said. Dave and Andi excused themselves a few moments later to greet old friends in the crowd. That left Joe and Sue Ellen with brief seconds of isolation amid the hundreds of guests.

"I'm glad you came," he said quietly.

"Me, too. The ceremony was so well done. And so moving. I got a little teary-eyed when all your troops marched past you and whipped their arms up in a last salute."

"So did I," he admitted with a sheepish grin, "but how about we keep that just between you and me?"

"My lips are sealed."

His glance dropped to her mouth and lingered a few seconds. When he met her gaze again, the gleam in his gold-brown eyes put a sudden hitch in Sue Ellen's breath.

"Not too tightly, I hope." His breath warming her cheek, he leaned down to murmur in her ear. "I think you should know that I…"

"Yo, Goodwin!"

The bluff greeting came with a hearty backslap that staggered Joe forward a half step.

"'Bout time you hung it up, you old buzzard."

With a smile that promised they'd finish their colloquy later, Joe slid a casual arm around Sue Ellen's waist and introduced her to a big bear of a man he'd served with in Afghanistan.

Their exchange of good-natured insults gathered an audience that gradually grew to a crowd. Sue Ellen laughed until her sides hurt at what she was sure were grossly exaggerated—and carefully expunged—tales of missions gone hilariously awry. All the while she remained acutely conscious of Joe's arm.

The embrace was so loose, so damned casual. She'd be a fool to read too much into it. Yet she caught more than one speculative glance aimed her way from Joe's friends and acquaintances.

When the crowd shifted, she also caught a glimpse of Rose standing next to Karen Duchek and her family. Sue Ellen's heart sank at the dark thundercloud on her protégée's face.

Oh, God! What now?

With a murmured "excuse me," she eased out of Joe's hold.

"Hi, guys."

Her easy greeting included Rose and the Duchecks. Like the other military present, Staff Sergeant Jerry Duchek was in dress blues decorated with a rack of ribbons and the badges signifying his branch and specialty. His two sons stair-stepped in height and age and shared their mother's bright copper hair.

"Great party, isn't it?" Sue Ellen said brightly.

Sergeant Duchek and his wife heartily agreed. Rose folded her arms and kept silent. Swallowing a sigh, Sue Ellen addressed her directly.

"Did you find the punch?"

"Yeah, I did."

Her glance shot across the room. Sue Ellen followed it to a table draped in red, white and blue bunting. A massive sheet cake decorated with Chief Master Sergeant's stripes and the insignia of Special Tactics held place of honor at one end. At the other was a sparkling crystal punch bowl.

And standing a few feet from the bowl, Sue Ellen saw with a silent groan, was Rafe Smith with a gorgeous redhead plastered against his side. Well, that explained the thundercloud.

With a sharp pang of sympathy for Rose's crushed hopes, Sue Ellen covered the awkward moment with small talk.

"That's a gorgeous dress, Karen. I love the lace."

"Do you?"

Pleasure lighting her face, Andi's ginger-haired assistant manager smoothed her hands over the antique lace ruffles cascading from her scooped neckline.

"I added this collar myself. I thought both the dress and I needed a little jazzing up."

Her youngest took instant exception to the self-deprecating comment. "You don't need jazzing, Mom. You *always* look good."

"Thanks, Ben."

Sergeant Duchek echoed his son's endorsement. "I second that."

"I third it," the oldest Duchek boy added in what was obviously a family ritual. Suddenly, his face scrunched.

"Avast, maties!" Ben gave his best imitation of a pirate's cackle. "Stand back or be blown away!"

The older boy whipped up an arm just in time to cover a monster sneeze.

"Thar he blows!" his kid brother sang gleefully.

"Ben, for heaven's sake!" Karen shook her head in exasperation. "Stop announcing every one of Kevin's sneezes to the world."

"Yeah, you dumb twerp." Face red, eyes watering, the older boy lowered his arm.

"It's his allergies," Karen explained to Sue Ellen. "They kick in every year about this time. The dust swirling through the hangar didn't help. We wanted to at least put in an appearance at the reception, but we need to take Kevin home pretty quick and turn on his air filter."

"Aw, Mom, you and Dad don't have to stay home 'n' miss the dinner 'cause of me."

His father laid a hand on his shoulder. "It's no big deal, son."

"But you said you really wanted to go to this Othello place. And Mom got all dressed up 'n' everything."

"We'll go another time."

"I'll stay with them."

The gruff offer came from Rose. She responded to the surprise it generated with a shrug.

"I looked after the kids at home all the time. If all Kevin needs is to breathe filtered air, I can stay with him and Ben."

Karen responded with a warm smile. "That's really sweet of you, but I couldn't let you miss the dinner at Othello's."

Rose zinged another quick glance across the room.

"I already decided I wasn't going," she said with careless nonchalance. "Too many old people. I'd rather hang with Kevin and Ben."

Karen had observed Rose at work for a week now and had no qualms about trusting the teen with her boys, but she gave her a last out.

"Are you sure you don't mind?"

"I'm sure." Deliberately, Rose turned her back on the refreshment table. "Do you guys have Xbox?"

"Xbox and Nintendo *and* PlayStation Two."

While Kevin and Ben recited a long list of the video games in their personal collections, Jerry Ducheck assured Sue Ellen he'd drive Rose home later that evening.

"Or she kin sleep over," Ben suggested. "I always beat Kevin too easy. I need more competition."

His eagerness for fresh blood won a smile from his intended victim. "Think I'm that good?"

"You can't be any worse," he returned, grinning. "Me 'n' Kev can sleep on the couch 'n' you can have our room. That way you 'n' mom can drive into the bookstore together tomorrow."

"Got it all planned, have you?"

Advising his son to back off, Sergeant Duchek herded the boys toward the door while Sue Ellen made a quick request of Rose.

"Call and let me know if you decide to stay over, okay?"

"Yeah, okay."

As she watched Rose and the Ducheks weave their way through the crowd, Sue Ellen felt like a kid let out of school early. She had a whole evening of adult company ahead of her. Maybe a whole night. No forced, one-sided conversations. No grudging, monosyllabic replies to her questions. Just good food, a full-bodied wine and scintillating company.

And Joe.

Who, Sue Ellen mused with a considering glance in his direction, seemed intent on making up for his four days of silence.

Not that she was counting.

SEVERAL HOURS LATER she was feeling considerably mellowed by two glasses of primo Chianti, veal Tuscan simmered to perfection and an evening filled with laughter. Joe's insistence that he would drive her back to the 7-Eleven to pick up her Mustang added to the tingling sensations thrumming just under her skin. It was only a short drive along U.S. 98, with the moon-washed Intercoastal

Waterway shimmering through the neon lights of motels, restaurants and touristy gift shops, but Sue Ellen was in no hurry for the ride to end.

Resting her head against the high seatback of his Ford 150 truck, she slanted him a sideways glance. He'd shed his uniform jacket and tie before appearing at the trendy Italian restaurant, as had most of the military personnel. Relaxed and comfortable in his short-sleeved, open-necked air force shirt, he steered through the night.

"Why didn't you call me?"

Sue Ellen hadn't intended to voice the question aloud, but now that it was out, she wanted an answer.

"I had planned to."

Tapping her nails on the armrest, she waited for him to follow through on that provocative statement.

"But?" she finally prompted.

"But we'd just spent three pretty intense weeks together. I decided to give you some space in the hope that the cliché proved true."

"The one about absence making the heart grow fonder?" Her nails drummed the armrest again. "So you weren't just wrapping up Phase One or getting ready for your retirement? This was a deliberate move?"

"Part of a carefully thought-out campaign," he admitted, angling her a quick look. "Did it work?"

Hell, yes, it had worked.

Sue Ellen supposed she should be pissed that he'd played her like a secondhand guitar but couldn't quite work up the steam. She was feeling too mellow, and too smug now that she knew he'd orchestrated an entire campaign.

"Let's just say you piqued my interest."

"That's not all I intend to pique."

"'Scuse me?"

"I hadn't planned to make my next move this soon, but I'd be a fool not to take advantage of the opportunity that dropped into my lap tonight."

His grin was slow, predatory and all male.

"Jerry Duchek told me he was driving Rose back to your place. I thought we might swing by mine for a nightcap."

Small, hot cinders sparked just under Sue Ellen's skin. Everything that was female in her wanted to murmur a husky yes. To her intense annoyance, her conscience got in the way.

"Before I agree to a nightcap, I think I should remind you that I'm seeing someone else on a more or less regular basis."

"I'm fully aware of that. Bill Steadman is one of the good guys."

"You know him?"

"Not personally, but any air commando worth his salt conducts a careful reconnoiter of the area of operations before finalizing his insertion strategy."

She should have guessed he'd scoped Crash out. It certainly wouldn't have been difficult to do. They both belonged to the relatively small, closed fraternity of Special Ops.

"And it doesn't bother you that Bill and I are, uh, involved?"

"It did, for about five minutes. Then I figured any man who hasn't put his brand on you after a year of 'more or less' had to take his chances."

"There you go again." Caught between amusement and exasperation, Sue Ellen shook her head. "Didn't we already have one discussion about territorial rights and living in the wrong century?"

"We did. Best I recall, we didn't reach consensus."

"There's no consensus required. I make my own decisions, Joe."

"So what did you decide about a nightcap?"

What she'd decided was that she didn't want her precious hours of freedom to end just yet. She'd spent every evening for almost a month in Rose's company. The sense of having slipped her leash was too heady to quash.

"I could do with a Baileys on the rocks."

"One Baileys coming up."

With a flick of the directional signals, he made a smooth lane change.

JOE LIVED IN A COMMUNITY of older, ranch-style homes that had suddenly become upscale when developers carved a championship golf course out of the sand and scrub pine surrounding it.

New million-dollar homes were scattered among the more established residences, many of which had For Sale signs in the front yard. Sue Ellen didn't doubt the owners stood to make a heck of a profit on their original investment.

"How long have you lived here?" she asked as he pulled into the driveway of a brick-fronted bungalow.

"Fourteen months this time around, a little over three years altogether since I bought the place back in '89."

"You were smart to hang on to it all these years. Looks as if your neighborhood got hit by the latest wave of golf-community development."

"More like a tsunami than a wave. They're putting up new houses as fast as they can bulldoze the old ones." Retrieving his service dress uniform jacket from the back seat, he came around to open her door. "I've received offers for this place that range from the unbelievable to the absurd."

"Are you going to sell?"

"Maybe. I haven't decided yet."

Ushering her to the paneled den at the rear of the house, he tossed his jacket and tie over the back of the sofa and made for the walk-in bar. On the way, he flipped the switch on a high-tech disk player. The raspy rhythm of Louis Armstrong's classic "Blueberry Hill" provided a counterpoint to the plink of ice hitting glass.

Sue Ellen used the brief interlude to take a look around. The furnishings were man-size and mostly leather. The decor reflected a career spent in the far corners of the world. A display of colorful Thai batiks decorated one wall. What looked like Somalian masks and spears bristled above the bar. The massive, oval-shaped coffee table was made of Turkish hammered brass, set off by an eight-by-twelve Turkish area rug. Its rich jewel colors were reflected in the plasma TV screen mounted above a narrow table containing an array of exquisitely carved Southwestern kachinas.

What drew her, though, were the bookshelves running the length of the south wall. One contained a desk unit housing a slick laptop and all-in-one printer/copier/scanner/fax. The rest of the shelves were crammed with books and folders and bound papers. She spotted a fat volume titled *Constructing Frames of Reference*, with the daunting subtitle that read *An Analytical Method for Archaeological Theory-Building Using Hunter-Gatherer and Environmental Sets*. Other tomes dealt with the Early Mississippian culture and the Trail of Tears.

What was missing, she noted as she surveyed the crowded shelves, was the usual I-love-me display found in so many military offices and homes. There were no plaques, no photos with VIPs, no array of squadron patches or souvenir aircraft parts. Nothing to indicate Joe had spent the past twenty-six years inserting himself and his small, lethal teams into dangerous hot spots around the world.

"Here you are."

"Thanks." Smiling, she tipped her brandy snifter of creamy liqueur to his glass of Scotch. "Here's to Joe Goodwin's personal STEP program."

"Maybe you'd better tell me what my personal program entails before I drink to it."

"Sunshine, Tranquillity, Ease and Prosperity. After twenty-six years in Special Ops, I'd say you were due a hefty dose of all four."

"I won't argue with that."

The Baileys went down like a mocha milkshake. Since it was coming on top of two glasses of wine, Sue Ellen took only a measured sip before accepting Joe's invitation to shed her linen jacket and kick off her spike heels. Considerably more relaxed, she curled up at one end of the sofa. He sank into the cushions at the other end.

"Do you think you'll miss the military?" she asked, taking a delicate lick at the creamy liqueur rimming the snifter. "Stupid question. Of course you will."

"It's been my whole life up to now, but I'm ready for the program you just described."

Actually, ease and tranquillity didn't figure anywhere on Joe's radar screen at the moment. Not after watching Sue Ellen's tongue do its thing.

Christ! The woman twisted him into knots faster than any female he'd stumbled across in his forty plus years. Did she have any idea of the kink she put in his gut? If she didn't, she soon would.

"I know about Bill Steadman," he said. "Tell me about your ex-husbands."

"Why? They're history."

"True, but that history made you the woman you are today."

The look that came into her lavender eyes was amused and just a touch wary. Good. The last thing Joe wanted was for her to feel safe *or* complacent around him.

"What is this? Part of your campaign strategy?"

"Absolutely. I wouldn't want to make the same mistakes with you they did."

"Ha! You couldn't! One was a jerk, the other a pathological liar."

Downing a swallow of the Glenmorangie single malt he'd picked up during a NATO exercise in northern Scotland last year, Joe savored its bite and the satisfaction of knowing that she was here, in his lair.

"Now you have to tell me. How did someone with your smarts hook up with a jerk and a liar?"

Sighing, she straightened her legs and leaned more comfortably against the sofa arm. Joe couldn't let the opportunity pass. Setting aside his glass, he hitched her feet into his lap and massaged one instep.

"I didn't know Charlie was a jerk when I met him. He was a senior at the University of Georgia, on an air force ROTC scholarship. I was a silly sophomore who fell head over hormones in love. So I quit school and followed him from base to base for seven years."

"Who got the seven-year itch," he asked, "you or him?"

"He did. God, that feels good!"

She wiggled her other foot to get his attention. Obediently, Joe went to work on that one. Her skin was warm through her nylons, the arch high and delicate.

"It took me another seven years to finish my undergraduate and graduate degrees," she continued, "but by then I'd landed a job with DOL and they had great tuition-assistance programs. I worked days, went to school at night and moved whenever a job opportunity presented itself."

"Sounds like you went through some tough years."

"They weren't so bad. I enjoyed school and loved my work. Still do. Andi and I stayed friends through all those years, which really helped when I needed someone to talk to, and I met a few interesting men along the way."

Joe bet she had.

"I was living in D.C. when someone introduced me to Ex Number Two at a cocktail party." Grimacing, she took another sip of Baileys. "He owned an art gallery and was really into the whole opening-night-at-the-Kennedy-Center scene. I didn't find out until later that at various times he'd also held part interest in a Napa Valley winery, a racing stable in Kentucky and a travel agency in Atlanta. Most, I might add, financed by ex-wives he'd neglected to mention. I started to get suspicious when he hit me up for a loan to keep the gallery afloat a mere week before the wedding."

She hadn't worked the disgust and anger over that mistake out of her system yet. Joe could feel it in the tension knotting the cords in her ankle.

"Relax." He kept his rhythm steady and his hold firm. "Everyone makes mistakes. At least you had the good sense to extricate yourself from yours."

"Not before the gallery went under, unfortunately. I ended up paying the bastard alimony until he reeled in his next fish. Last I heard he was playing the wealthy restaurateur in Chicago."

His hands moved higher, kneading her calf while he calculated how much longer it would take him to have her out of her panty hose. Not long, judging by her small mewl of pleasure.

"What about you?" she asked as his fingers worked her flesh. "How did you manage to avoid marital mistakes?"

"I came close a few times."

Joe tried to summon the face of the woman he'd fallen so hard for as a young airman, but she was lost in the mist of time. He didn't have any trouble visualizing the teacher he'd planned to marry some years back, until she decided she didn't want a husband who was gone more than he was home.

"What happened?"

"The gods of war intervened both times. You finished with that drink?"

Blinking at the abrupt change of subject, she held up the snifter and sloshed its contents. "Not yet."

"Take a chug, then, so we can get it out of the way."

The wariness came back into her eyes. "Out of the way of what?"

Plucking the snifter from her fingers, he set it next to his highball glass. She was half prone now, her legs draped over his. The perfect angle for him to grasp her hips and slide her onto the cushions.

"Joe…"

The low warning brought a smile and a promise.

"We'll stop, Sue Ellen, whenever you say the word."

CHAPTER 14

She could stop him.

Anytime she said the word.

Sue Ellen didn't need Joe's husky promise to know he wouldn't push her where she didn't want to go.

The problem was, she wanted to go *exactly* where he was pushing her. Deep into the leather cushions, with his body angling into hers at all the right pressure points. She knew her skirt had hiked up, felt his knee push it up farther as he distributed his weight so he wouldn't crush her. The press of that hard, muscled leg against the inside of her thighs kicked Sue Ellen's pulse into a wild gallop.

Okay, she told herself. All right. She needed to do this. His first kiss had caught her off guard. She hadn't expected it, still wasn't sure whether surprise or shock or a combination of both had stirred such a fierce heat in her.

This time, she was in control. This time she'd call the shots. And when she ended this kiss, she'd know whether she should call Crash and break it off between them.

Except it didn't take until the end of the kiss. It didn't even require mouth-to-mouth contact. When Joe slid a hand under her nape to hold her steady and her eyes met his, she knew. Deep inside, she knew. She wanted his kiss— she wanted *him*—with a primal, instinctive need that went beyond desire, beyond mere hunger.

Then his mouth molded hers. The kiss wasn't polite or gentle or the least tentative. He took, and she gave. Eagerly. Greedily. Her arms locked behind his neck, her body taut and straining against his.

This is the way it should be, a distant corner of her mind acknowledged. The way she suspected it would always be with Joe. Not a game played with teasing, provocative rules. Not a coquettish dance accented with pretty words and seductive strokes. This was basic, elemental and so powerful it left Sue Ellen trembling.

It also scared the crap out of her.

She'd never surrendered so completely, or felt so…so consumed. By one damned kiss!

Yanking her arms down, she wedged them against his chest. Her breath was a hoarse rasp when she broke contact with his mouth.

"Joe! Wait!"

He levered up a few inches, just enough for her to see

the hunger stamped all over his rugged face. As she watched, hunger gave way to fierce satisfaction.

"Knocked you for a loop, huh?"

She wasn't ready to admit that. Joe spared her the necessity.

"Me, too," he confessed.

Sue Ellen's heart turned over in her chest. Later, she would swear she felt it give a painful thump and rolled right over. The ache deepened when he feathered his thumb across her tender, swollen lips.

"If we don't stop now," she murmured, struggling to cap the fire still searing her blood, "we won't stop, period. I can't do that to Crash. I have to…"

Dragging in a deep, shuddering breath, she said a silent farewell to the man who'd warmed her heart and her bed for all these months. Whatever happened—or didn't happen—with Joe, she knew she couldn't continue to use Crash as a stand-in stud. Although he seemed perfectly content in that role, he deserved better.

"I have to end it with him first," she finished on a ragged note.

Joe blew out a long breath. "That's what I was afraid you'd say."

He dropped another kiss on her mouth before levering

up and off the sofa with a speed that left Sue Ellen feeling suddenly naked.

"Let's get you home so you can do what needs to be done."

Suiting his actions to his words, he pulled her to her feet and bent to scoop up her shoes. Spike heels in hand, he grabbed her linen jacket.

"It's only a little after ten D.C. time. You can call Steadman tonight. Did you bring a purse? Yeah, here it is. Let's go."

As he hustled her down the hall, Sue Ellen couldn't decide whether to burst into laughter or whap him with her bag. Laughter won out…until they approached the front door.

"Joe, for Pete's sake! At least let me put on my shoes before you drag me outside."

HER MUSTANG WAS STILL AT the 7-Eleven where she'd parked it what now seemed like a week ago.

Sometime in the past five or six hours her life had taken an entirely new direction. Feeling as though she was caught in the swift-flowing current of the Blackwater, Sue Ellen gathered her things while Joe came around to open her door.

He walked her to the Mustang and waited until she'd

fished her keys out of her purse to curl a knuckle under her chin. Tilting her face to his, he issued a gruff order.

"Call him tonight, Sue Ellen."

Enough was enough. She could only be pushed so far.

"You need to back off, Joe."

"I just did, back there at the house, and it damned near killed me."

He followed the admission with a kiss that took some of the bite from Sue Ellen's voice, but she stuck to her guns.

"I've got to handle this my way."

"Agreed. Just handle it soon, will you, or I'll be walking with a permanent limp."

ROSE WAS UPSTAIRS IN HER room when she made it back to the condo. The muted sounds of the TV drifted from under the guest room door as Sue Ellen kicked off her shoes once again and carried them up the stairs.

With so much on her mind, she *really* wanted to just shout out that she was home and retreat into her own bedroom. She needed to think through the phone call she had to make, choose just the right words. But she knew how upset Rose had been at seeing Rafe Smith with that luscious redhead. Her pesky conscience demanded she at least check on the girl.

Forcing herself to bypass her own room, she rapped on the guest room door. "Rose? May I come in?"

She took the inarticulate sound that drifted through the panel for an affirmative and cracked the door open. Rose lay sprawled on her stomach, her chin on her folded hands. Minus the eye makeup and dangly earrings she looked younger, less like a ripe young woman and more like a girl.

"How was your evening?"

"Okay."

"Did the boys wear you down?"

"No."

Sue Ellen took a deep breath and moved into the guest room. It was as neat as always, with no scattered clothes in sight and Rose's few possessions aligned precisely on the nightstand and dresser.

"I'm sorry you missed dinner at Othello's." She plopped down on the edge of the bed, forcing Rose to swing her legs to one side. "The place is really snazzy."

With an exaggerated sigh, the teen hit the remote and killed the TV. "That's what Karen said."

"So what did you and the boys do all evening?"

"Video games, mostly." She rolled upright, her glance widening. "And what did *you* do this evening?"

Sue Ellen shot a glance at the mirror over the dresser and barely suppressed a yelp. Her hair stood in messy spikes, compliments of the hands Joe had thrust through it. She'd been so preoccupied on the drive home she'd forgotten to refresh her lipstick, and her blouse now sported almost as many wrinkles as her linen skirt.

"Jerry said Joe drove you to get your car," Rose commented slyly. "Sure took you guys a long time."

"We went by his place for a nightcap."

"Uh-huh."

"Okay, we indulged in a little more than a drink. Just kisses," she added hastily, jamming a hand through the spikes to flatten them. "Correction, make that one kiss."

"You come home looking like you got run over by a freight train after one kiss?" Rose whistled, long and low. "Joe must be *really* good at it."

Sue Ellen gave a strangled laugh and dropped her arm. "He is, dammit."

She had Rose's full attention now. With a look of grudging admiration, the teen curled her legs under her. "I'm impressed. Crash *and* Joe? You sure you can handle two hotties like that?"

Especially at her advanced age. Rose didn't actually say the words, but the implication came through loud and clear. Hiding a wry smile, Sue Ellen nodded.

"It would be a challenge, but I think I could manage it…if I played the game that way. I don't. I prefer to limit myself to one hottie at a time."

"Probably a smart move in this instance," Rose agreed. "I can't see Joe standing in line, waiting his turn. He'd want it all or nothing."

"Mmmm, I pretty much got that impression."

"So which one is the keeper, or haven't you decided?"

She'd decided but had yet to cut the cord. Loyalty to Crash made her hesitate, which prompted a shrug from Rose.

"Well, I know which one I'd keep."

"Which?"

"Joe," she said without hesitation. "Hands down."

"Really? Why?"

"Crash is okay and seems to have it all together, but Joe is the one I'd call if I was in trouble. He's…" Frowning, she searched for the right word. "He's solid."

From the mouths of babes, Sue Ellen thought, marveling at how precisely Rose had nailed it.

Crash made her feel young and alive and sexy as hell. With Joe, she felt as though she could climb a sheer, rocky precipice or weather the worst storm. That he also made her feel sexy as hell was icing on the cake.

"As it happens," she admitted, "I agree with you. I don't have any idea where things will go between Joe and me. After tonight, though, I know I need to end it with Crash. I hate to do it by phone, but…"

"But he'll be gone for weeks," Rose finished with a knowing nod, "and Joe wants more than a kiss. Just say the word, Sue Ellen, whenever you want me to drive over to the mall and hang for a few hours."

Oh, sure! Like that was going to happen. She might be chafing a little at her loss of privacy, but she hoped she had more couth than to banish a teenager so she could get it on with a lover.

"I'll keep that in mind," she said dryly as she pushed off the bed. "Now I'd better call Crash before it gets too late."

Or she chickened out.

Flopping down on her belly, Rose clicked the remote. "Good luck."

"Thanks."

HER NUMBER MUST HAVE POPPED up on caller ID. Crash answered his cell phone on the second ring.

"Hey, gorgeous. I hope you're calling to tell me you can't get to sleep until you hear the sound of my voice."

Wincing, Sue Ellen jettisoned all the lead-ins she'd practiced during the drive home to ease into the conversation.

"Not exactly."

Crash picked up on her cautious tone. "You don't sound like yourself, S.E. Are you okay?"

"I'm fine."

Not true. She was miserable. She hated hurting a man she liked and respected as much as Bill Steadman.

"It's just… Well… I've been thinking about us."

"You have, huh?"

God, she wished there was an easy way to do this!

"You know how much I enjoy being with you. This past year has been wonderful."

Was that lame, or what? Thoroughly disgusted with herself, Sue Ellen plowed ahead.

"The thing is, neither of us went into this relationship intending for it to become permanent."

Her voice gentled. She was walking treacherous ground by bringing up the subject they rarely discussed.

"You're still grieving for your wife, Crash. I know in my heart I could never replace her."

He greeted that with a silence that stretched for several, interminable seconds.

"I think what you're trying to tell me," he said finally, "is that you don't want to replace her."

She winced again at the sudden chill in his voice but gave him an honest answer. "No, I don't. I never have. And you don't want me to."

This pause was longer, but ended on a sigh that chased away the coldness.

"You're right, Sue Ellen. I buried my wife, and you made

it clear right from the start that you weren't in the market for another husband. You want to tell me who's changed your mind?"

"Oh, Crash! I'm not to the husband stage yet. I'm not even sure I like the man half the time."

"You're dumping me for someone you're not sure you like? Who is this guy?"

"Joe Goodwin. He runs the STEP program."

"*Chief* Joe Goodwin?"

"Yes. Do you know him?"

"By reputation."

She held her breath, waiting for him to expand on that provocative statement.

"Doesn't do a lot for my ego to get cut out by a grizzled chief fifteen or twenty years my senior," he drawled. "If it had to happen, though, you could do a helluva lot worse than Joe Goodwin."

Relieved, Sue Ellen sank into the decorator pillows mounded against the headboard. "I'm *so* sorry to break this to you over the phone. I know I should have waited for you to get back."

"Would it have been easier face-to-face?"

"No. I'd still feel awful."

"Yeah, well, you should."

The tart reply told her his pride had indeed been dinged.

His relatively easy acceptance of his walking papers, on the other hand, suggested his heart would survive intact. Sue Ellen was grateful for that, if a little chagrined.

"I just thought you deserved to know before I… That is, before Joe and I…"

"I get the picture. Thanks for that, Sue Ellen."

She cradled the phone to her ear, thinking back over their months together. "We had some good times, didn't we?"

"That we did. We still could," he said, half joking, half serious. "If things don't work out with Goodwin, babe, you know how to reach me."

Okay, now he was going to make her cry.

"Yes, I do. Bye, Crash."

"Bye, Sue Ellen."

Sniffling, she punched End Call and tossed the phone at the foot of the bed. A nasty voice inside her head shouted that she was nuts to toss aside a man who knew exactly what buttons to press to make her purr with pleasure. A man every bit as content with their casual arrangement as she had been.

That same nasty voice warned that Joe wouldn't be as easy to handle. Not that she needed the warning. Goodwin had given her more than one glimpse of the me-Tarzan-you-Jane male lurking just inside his psyche.

Here, in the privacy of her bedroom, Sue Ellen could admit that a secret part of her thrilled to his blunt, uncomplicated view of the sexes. Every woman fantasized about being "claimed," as Joe had so inelegantly put it, by a rogue male. She was certainly no exception.

Fantasy was one thing, however. Holding her own against someone as smart, tough and uncompromising as Joe Goodwin was something else again.

If nothing else, she thought as she padded into the bathroom, the task should prove interesting.

SUE ELLEN LAID AWAKE for some time mulling over her decision and was still harboring a few doubts when she showered and dressed the next morning.

The scent of fresh-perked coffee wafting through the vents drew her downstairs. She didn't remember setting the timer last night. Maybe she'd gone through the motions while rehearsing her speech to Crash.

Or not.

The sight of Rose up, dressed and doodling on some sheets of paper at the kitchen table gave her a small jolt. Nothing compared to the one that hit when she remembered they had a meeting with the Blues that afternoon and hadn't yet come up with a design for the display. Swallowing a groan, she made for the coffee.

"'Morning, Rose. You're up early."

"You said we needed to work on the design before we meet with the team this afternoon, remember?"

"I do."

Now. Extracting a mug from the cupboard, Sue Ellen reached for the pot.

"Looks like you've come up with some ideas."

"A couple." Rose tapped her pencil on the paper, her glance speculative. "Did you talk to Crash last night?"

"Yes."

"How'd he take it?"

"Pretty well, all things considered."

There it was again, that tiny niggle of pique. What a bitch she was for wishing he'd at least pretended she'd dented his heart as well as his ego. Thoroughly annoyed with herself, Sue Ellen poured it black and straight into a mug.

"You know," Rose said with studied casualness, "I was thinking I might console the guy. If it didn't get you all bent out of shape."

Sue Ellen managed to keep from slopping hot coffee all over the counter. Heroically, she also managed to bite back the sharp retort that Rose was too damned young to console a major in the United States Air Force, even if said major had achieved his rank well ahead of his peers.

When she thought about it, Sue Ellen had to admit math worked against her. She was twelve years older than Crash. Crash was only eleven years Rose's senior. But those eleven years represented a gap the size of the Grand Canyon given where they all were in their lives. Then there was the slight matter of the sixteen-year-old being jailbait. Sue Ellen considered a number of responses before deciding the truth served best.

"I have to admit, I'm very uncomfortable with the idea of you hooking up with Crash."

She was prepared for an argument or a sulky scowl. Rose surprised her with a shrug.

"He's history, then. Are you having breakfast?"

"Just coffee."

"Want to look at these sketches while you drink it? I'm not sure how they'll translate to the computer-design program on your laptop."

Feeling as though she'd just cleared a major hurdle with several inches to spare, Sue Ellen carried her mug to the table.

SHE DIDN'T HIT THE NEXT hurdle until Monday morning, when she again found Rose up and waiting for her in the kitchen.

"The radio says it's going to be a beautiful day. Can we

put the top down on the Mustang for the drive in? Or I can wait until after I drop you off if it'll muss you up too much."

Gulping, Sue Ellen recalled her promise to let Rose ferry her to work this week. All part of the plan to build confidence and trust between them.

Except the ferry was a sleek, high-powered Mustang. Sue Ellen's personal muscle machine. The sports car ate up the pavement like a tiger on the prowl, and that was in Drive. When it kicked into Overdrive, the thing took off like a F-15 hitting the afterburner. Rose had demonstrated cool confidence behind the wheel under Sue Ellen's watchful eye. Would she do as well when she slipped her leash?

To combat the sudden sinking in her stomach, Sue Ellen trotted out the platitudes. Trust was a two-way street. You had to earn confidence to receive it. One "borrowed" car did not another make.

Despite the stern self-lectures, she wavered between doubt and reluctance to say goodbye to Rose and the Mustang during most of the way in to Pensacola. When they pulled up at the plaza in front of her office building, she fiddled around and delayed exiting the car.

"You're working until four this afternoon, right?"

"Right. I go in at eleven, get off at four."

"Plan to pick me up at five. If something comes up and I need to stay longer, I'll call you."

"Okay."

"You've got your cell phone?"

Rose patted the purse wedged between her and the console. "Right here."

"And the money I gave you for gas?"

"In with the phone."

"Okay. Well… I'll see you later."

Feeling like a mother sending her child off into the unknown, Sue Ellen swung out of the low-slung convertible and thudded the door shut behind her. She stood there, chewing on the inside of her lip, as her protégée gave a nonchalant wave and pulled away from the curb.

ROSE CRUISED BACK OVER the Pensacola Bay Bridge with her hair whipping in the wind and her blood pumping to the rhythm of the tires singing on the pavement. The long, raucous honk she got from the trucker who whizzed past earned him a grin and a toss of her head.

God, this was sweet!

The Mustang handled like sugar candy. She hadn't been able to open her up during her short, unsupervised trips to the grocery store. The other times she'd been at the wheel, Sue Ellen had watched her like a hawk.

Too bad the traffic was so heavy on this stretch of U.S. 98. Rose itched to put some weight on the accelerator. The urge intensified when she spotted the blue-and-white sign announcing the entrance ramp for I-10 one mile ahead.

She didn't have to be at work for hours. She could hit the Interstate and go for fifty miles in either direction before turning back.

Or *not* turn back and go forever.

The craving to escape was there, inside her. It was always there, although it didn't gnaw at her as viciously as it had a month or so ago. These weeks with Sue Ellen had blunted some of the raw animal instinct to get away and find a safe hole to burrow into.

Blunted, but not killed.

Another blue-and-white sign appeared in the distance. A half a mile to the entrance to I-10.

Sweat dampened Rose's palm. Her breath got shorter. Her heart hammering, she gripped the wheel with clammy fists.

CHAPTER 15

Sue Ellen paced the sidewalk in front of her office building and checked her watch for the third time.

Five-ten.

Three minutes later than the last time she checked.

Shifting her briefcase to her other hand, she swiped her hair off her forehead. There really wasn't any need for her to feel so twitchy. Rosé was only ten minutes late. It just *seemed* longer because Sue Ellen had rushed a conference call to get downstairs before five so her chauffeur wouldn't have to circle the block too many times.

Her hand itched to reach into her purse for her cell phone, but she resisted, just as she'd resisted the urge to call the bookstore at eleven—and one and three—to make sure Rose had made it to work.

Trust was a two-way street.

You had to impart confidence to receive it.

Where the heck was she?

Okay, the traffic was really bad. Bumper-to-bumper

heading toward the bridge. Exhaust fumes wrinkled Sue Ellen's nose and added to the humid summer heat plastering her cream-and-gold print blouse to her back.

Sticky and sweaty and *not* nervous, she was checking her watch again when two short honks whipped her head around.

"Thank God," she muttered as the Mustang separated from the traffic and glided to the curb. A quick inspection revealed no dents, dings or scratches.

Refusing to acknowledge the relief coursing through her, Sue Ellen tossed her briefcase in the back and dropped into the passenger seat. The sun-baked leather burned right through the thin material of her skirt.

"Ouch!"

Back arched, she raised her butt off the seat. Beside her, a windblown and pink-cheeked Rose did the same. Yanking a folded towel from under her, she handed the thick terry cloth to Sue Ellen.

"The hot leather scorched my rear, too. I had to borrow this from the shop. Next time I'll put the top up or find some shade to park in."

"Good idea."

Waiting until Sue Ellen's bottom was shielded and her seat belt in place, Rose shot a quick look over her shoulder and rejoined the traffic stream.

"Sorry I'm late. They started some roadwork on 98 East,

just the other side of the bridge. I was going to call when I cleared the orange cones but you said not to use the cell phone while at the wheel."

"I'm glad you didn't. I'd much rather you were a few minutes late than wrapped around a telephone pole or bridge abutment. So how did work go?"

"Good." She thought about that for a moment. "Great, actually."

Sue Ellen jumped on the superlative. Rose didn't use them often, if at all!

"Why great?"

"Those books Andi ordered, the ones Joe and Roger recommended on Native American tribes of the Southeast, came in today. I spent most of the afternoon flipping through the pages before I shelved them."

A hint of excitement coloring her voice, Rose shot her passenger a quick look.

"You know the design we worked up for the Blues' community project?"

"How could I forget? We spent all Saturday morning translating your sketches into the computer."

They had struggled with a design program that would allow variation of placement while maintaining spatial differentiation for each object. Sue Ellen sincerely hoped Rose wasn't about to ask her to go through that exercise in frustration again.

"One of the books Andi ordered is a big glossy volume that catalogs the Smithsonian's Native American collection. In the book, they display masks on an overlay you can superimpose on a human figure."

"They do, huh?"

The guarded response earned a grin from Rose. A real, honest-to-goodness grin. Sue Ellen felt as though she'd just been awarded first prize at the county fair.

"Andi let me bring the book home to show you. It wouldn't be too hard to add the outline of a human form to our display, would it?"

"I don't *think* so. We'll take a look at it when we get home."

Gingerly, Sue Ellen let her shoulder blades make contact with the seat back. Its heat was bearable now, kind of like a hot-rocks spa treatment. The wind blasting through the convertible provided enough relief from the sun for her to relax and enjoy cruising across the Bay Bridge…until Rose reopened a touchy subject, that is.

"I wanted to talk to you again about taking the kids for pizza tomorrow."

"I thought we agreed to wait until the weekend."

"We did. Sort of. But I've been thinking…"

"Rose…"

"Just listen, okay?"

Weaving around a slow-moving vehicle, she cut back into her lane with careful skill.

"I'm off all day tomorrow. I thought I'd call Joan and ask her to bring the kids and meet me at the pizza place." Her mouth twisted. "If I tell her it's my treat, she'll jump at it."

"That sounds like a doable workaround," Sue Ellen said after mulling the proposal over. "That way we wouldn't have to borrow Andi's SUV to pick up the kids."

And Rose wouldn't have to go back to the Scotts' house to face her tormentor. Neither of them mentioned that matter, but it remained front and center in Sue Ellen's mind as Rose flicked her another glance.

"There's only one problem. Donny and Nick are in day camp for the summer. They don't get out until four-thirty. I'll ask Joan if she can take them out early so we finish in time for me to pick you up at five. If not…"

"If not, I can put in a few extra hours at work."

Trust, Sue Ellen chanted silently. Confidence. Two-way streets. The gratitude that leaped into Rose's eyes seemed to underscore the truth of the clichés.

"You don't mind? You're sure?"

"I'm sure."

They drove in companionable silence for a few hundred

yards. Sue Ellen was contemplating slipping in a Jimmy Hendrix CD so they could rock their way across the bridge when Rose dropped another suggestion.

"There's another option, you know."

"Option for what?"

"For tomorrow evening. Instead of working late, you could let Joe take you out for dinner." She waggled her eyebrows. "Or whatever."

Nothing like having a sixteen-year-old pimp for you, Sue Ellen thought ruefully.

"Joe's called you since you broke up with Crash, hasn't he?"

"You know he did. You answered the phone last night, when I was in the shower, and took the message for me to call back."

"Yeah, but you didn't."

"Yes, I did. This morning, from my office."

"Well? Aren't you going to tell me his reaction to the Crash thing?"

"No." She softened the blunt negative with a smile. "That conversation was private and, uh, slightly X-rated."

Rose's grin popped out again. Sue Ellen wished the girl knew how pretty she was when her face lit up and her eyes sparkled like that.

"So here's your chance to follow up on that conversation. I say you should go for it, Sue Ellen."

"You do, huh?"

"I do. You'd be nuts to let someone like Joe slip through your fingers."

THAT THOUGHT STAYED WITH Sue Ellen as she primped in front of the mirror in her office the following afternoon.

As Rose had predicted, Joan Scott had jumped on the offer of a free meal for her and the kids. Joe had done the same when Sue Ellen called to bum a ride home this evening and offered dinner at her favorite seafood restaurant in payment, except he'd countered with Chinese takeout at his place.

So here she was, as nervous as a high-schooler about to get it on with the king of cool. And get it on they would. Sue Ellen was long past the age of playing coy. She wanted Joe Goodwin with the same greedy hunger he wanted her. The only question was whether it would happen before or after the General Kao Sesame Chicken.

Before, she decided when she slid in beside Joe ten minutes later. Most definitely before! The man looked as good as he smelled.

Part of the tantalizing aroma wafted from the sacks stashed in the back seat. Most, however, was carried on the breeze blowing from the vents.

"Mmmm," Sue Ellen said, leaning toward Joe to sniff at the clean, tangy scent. "You smell wonderful. What is that?"

To her surprise and delight, a slow tide of red rose from the collar of his open-necked knit shirt.

"Armani. Something called Acqua diGio. I, uh, may have gone a little overboard with it. I don't usually use cologne."

"Let me guess," Sue Ellen said, laughing. "It draws gnats."

"That, and it makes me feel like I ought to be wearing a purple silk shirt and sporting a nose ring."

"So you think body piercing is only for the purple-shirt crowd?"

"Let me put it this way. My men knew damned well they'd better not report for duty with any form of metal stuck through them except a knife blade or a bayonet."

Suddenly, Sue Ellen's ridiculous schoolgirl jitters evaporated. Joe might possess vast expertise in wilderness survival, rescue ops and all other things military, but he could still learn a thing or two. And she was just the woman to teach him.

With a throaty laugh, she issued a challenge. "Care to put your money where your macho is?"

"Huh?"

"Five bucks says your outlook on body piercing changes after tonight."

Wrenching his gaze from the road, Joe raked her with a quick look.

"Well?" she purred, tiptoeing her fingers up his forearm. "Does Joey wanna bet or not?"

"Depends on whose body we're talking about piercing. And what part."

"You pays your money, you takes your chances. Are you in or not?"

"I'm in."

By the time they arrived at his place, Ellen had worked out her game plan. Plucking the sack of Chinese takeout from his hand, she deposited it on the counter dividing the den from the kitchen area. Then she backed him to the leather recliner his troops had presented him with at his retirement ceremony, put her hands on his chest and shoved.

"Sit. Say nothing. Do nothing."

Her plan called for music, any kind of music, but preferably something with an erotic beat. The bluesy sax that wailed through the speakers when she flipped on his CD player was perfect.

The next step required closing the drapes before clicking on the high-intensity reading lamp on his desk. That she angled so the beam bathed her midsection in white light when she took up a position in front of his chair. Picking up the beat of the sax, she began to sway her hips and tugged the tails of her blouse free of her skirt.

Joe's mind had been churning since Sue Ellen brought

up this body-piercing thing in the car. His puse went as crazy as his thoughts when she started on the buttons of her blouse.

What the hell was he going to see when she removed it?

He was ninety-nine-percent certain she hadn't pierced her nipples. No way he could have missed nipple rings all those times at camp when she was drenched in sweat or up to her armpits in river water. It was the one-percent uncertainty that got him instantly and painfully hard.

His hands were fisted by the second button. By the third, the vein in his temple throbbed. When the fourth gave, the pale lavender half bra she revealed made him salivate like one of Pavlov's dogs.

As if she'd read his mind, Sue Ellen shrugged out of her blouse and let it slither to the Turkish carpet. Curving her lips in a knowing smile, she cupped her breasts to deepen the shadowy cleavage.

"I can guess what you're thinking, big guy. Sorry to disappoint you. No metal here. It's all me."

"And you think that disappoints me?"

Her hands went to her slowly gyrating hips. Palming down her thighs, she gripped her skirt.

Still smiling, she inched the fabric up. Her garter belt was the same lacy lilac as her bra and just about did it for Joe.

He wanted to unhook those frilly garters and peel off her stockings almost as much as he wanted to drag her onto his lap and go around them.

But this was her show, and she was obviously enjoying the hell out of every twitch of his screaming muscles. So he kept his hands to himself as she swayed closer, her skirt hiked around her hips. Lifting a foot, she planted the spiked point of one heel on his knee.

"Shoes first," she murmured in a husky rasp. "Then the stockings."

As he planed her calf, Joe forgot he was supposed to be checking for extraneous metal objects and just let himself enjoy the smooth curve of flesh. It took some doing, but he managed to remove her stockings and garter belt without giving in to the urge to slide his hands under her bunched-up skirt, hook a finger in her briefs and drag them down, too.

"Okay, Joe." Easing away, she twisted her arms behind her back. "Here it comes. Ready?"

Erotic images rocketed through his mind. What in the *hell* was she going to show him?

His breath stuck mid-chest and stayed there as she worked the back zipper. Then the skirt slithered down to join her blouse, and Joe burst out laughing.

"That's your body piercing? That little twinkie in your belly button?"

"I'll have you know this twinkie is a one-and-a-third-carat, VVS2 diamond."

Rolling her tummy muscles, she bent to admire the sparkling stone.

"It used to be my engagement ring. From my second ex. I think it looks much better in my navel than on my finger, don't you?"

"Good grief, Sue Ellen! If anyone outside this room had *any* notion of the thoughts you put in my head, we'd both be in jail right now."

"That was the whole idea, fella. The anticipation got you revved and ready, didn't it?"

"I've been revved and ready, as you so delicately put it, since you called last night."

"Now that you mention it, so have I."

That was all Joe needed to hear. He came out of the recliner in a swift surge and scooped her into his arms.

His bedroom was dark, with only a faint gleam of sunlight filtering through the shutters. That was more than enough illumination for his gut to constrict at the picture Sue Ellen made after he'd dragged down the spread and laid her on the sheets.

She was perfect. All lustrous skin. Smooth curves. Seductive hollows. Joe had been hurting out there in the den, but watching her drape her arms above her head and smile a slow, languorous invitation damn near doubled him over. Dragging his shirt over his head, he tossed it aside and fumbled for his belt.

"Wait. Let me."

She came up on her knees, and he swallowed a groan when she reached for the buckle. By the time she had it open, he was gritting his teeth again. And when she leaned forward, her breath hot on the bare skin of his belly as she tugged at his zipper, Joe decided playtime was over.

Tumbling her to the sheets, he followed her down.

THE FIRST TIME WAS HARD and driving, with Sue Ellen's legs locked around Joe's and her gasps urging him on. He held on to his sanity long enough to remember a condom, but his brain shut down and his body took over when he kneed her thighs apart again and positioned himself between them.

The second time was slower, sweeter, with each of them taking time to touch and taste and tease. Sue Ellen could have spent hours exploring the hard ridges and smooth contours of Joe's body. The combination of warm skin, taunt tendon and the musky scent of their lovemaking, mixed with his expensive cologne, offered such a feast for her senses that she used every skill in her repertoire to delay the inevitable.

When the shattering climax finally came, it broke without warning. She'd straddled Joe, taking him into her with a slow, deliberate clench of vaginal muscles. She fully intended to ride him until he begged for mercy, but he was so big, and she was so hungry for him.

Leaning forward, she locked his hands in hers and had worked her hips only three or four times when the sudden spike of heat low in her belly exploded into bursts of blinding sensation.

Sue Ellen's head went back. Her spine arced. Groaning, she rode the orgasm and, with a last desperate play of muscle, took Joe with her.

When the wild ride was over, she collapsed in a boneless puddle onto his chest. She was still there, panting with pleasure, when a muted ping pierced her haze.

"Sounds like a cell phone."

The deep rumble worked its way up from the chest under her ear.

"Yours or mine?" Sue Ellen mumbled.

"Yours. Hang loose, I'll get it for you."

Good thing Joe could move, because she couldn't summon an ounce of anything that resembled energy. While she dragged a corner of the sheet over her bare butt, he padded into the other room. She had time to admire *his* bare butt on the way out, and his bare front when he returned.

The cell phone in his fist pinged again, louder and more insistently. Banishing the lascivious thoughts engendered by Joe's all-over tan, Sue Ellen took the phone and glanced at the liquid crystal display.

She didn't recognize the area code and number at first, until she remembered the preprogrammed cell phone she'd bought for Rose to carry with her. Flopping back on the pillows, she flipped up the lid.

"Hi, Rose. How was the pizza par—?"

"Sue Ellen! I… I'm in trouble. I need you!"

The panic lacing the girl's voice jerked Sue Ellen upright. A dozen potential disasters flashed through her head, from a Mustang with a crumpled front to a smoke-filled condo.

"What is it, Rose? What's happened?"

"I think… I think…"

Her voice broke on a dry, racking sob. Sue Ellen fought to keep hers from spiraling into a shriek.

"Rose! Take a deep breath. Tell me what happened."

"Oh, Sue Ellen!" The cry was a terrified, terrifying wail. "I think I killed him."

CHAPTER 16

Sue Ellen's heart stopped dead in her chest. With Rose's desperate wail ringing in her ears, she gripped the phone until her knuckles turned bone white.

"Who…?" She gulped, dragging air into her shocked lungs. "Who do you think you killed?"

"Pus Face. He was there. At the pizza place. He… He followed me when I left. Tried to… Tried to…"

The sobs came raw and fast now, choking off the words.

"Rose! You have to tell me what happened. Tell me where you are, if you're hurt. Wait! Hold on! Joe's right here. I'm going to put you on Speaker."

Frantic, Sue Ellen stabbed the tiny speaker button and held out the phone with shaking fingers. "Can you hear me?"

"Yes!"

"Tell us where you are, if you're hurt."

"I don't know where I am," Rose sobbed. "I tried to lose him. Took a bunch of turns. I'm on some back road and

he's…he's in a ditch. There's water, Sue Ellen! Deep water!
I can't get him out."

Joe took it from there. Calm. Strong. Authoritative.

"Slow down, Rose. Tell us if you're hurt or bleeding."

"No. I banged my head when the Mustang hit, but…but
there's no blood."

"Okay, here's what you're going to do. You stay on the
phone and keep this call open. Do you hear me?"

The answer was a rasping sob.

"I'm going to get on another phone and call 911. They'll
track your cell phone signal and vector in on your location.
It'll take a few minutes. Don't hang up. Just keep talking to
Sue Ellen. Do you understand?"

"Y…yes."

"I need your cell phone number. Do you have it memor-
ized?"

"No. I can… I can try to retrieve it."

"I wrote the number down," Sue Ellen interjected hastily.
"It's in my purse."

She thrust the phone at Joe and lunged off the bed and
almost tripped over the tangled sheet that came with her.
Cursing, she snatched the ends up and raced for the purse
she'd left in the den. By the time she'd fumbled the scribbled
phone number out of her wallet, Joe had somehow managed
to drag on his briefs and now stood right at her elbow.

"Okay, Rose. I'm giving the phone back to Sue Ellen. I'll tell you when we have a lock on your location. The police will most likely respond first, but we'll be right behind them."

AFTERWARD, SUE ELLEN WOULD swear she'd babbled into that cell phone for hours. She had no idea what she said, was sure she did a rotten job of smothering her own panic as she tried to calm a weeping, terrified Rose.

She almost broke down herself when Joe scribbled furiously on a pad, slammed down his house phone and took over the cell.

"We've got you, Rose. You're only about twelve miles from here. The police are on their way. We're leaving right now."

Sue Ellen was already scrambling into her clothes. She went for minimum coverage only. Skirt. Blouse. A pair of giant flip flops snatched from Joe's closet.

He pulled on jeans and a red knit shirt, then wasted what she considered precious moments lacing up a pair of boots until she remembered her hard-learned survival lessons. Always go in prepared for the worst.

In this case, she thought on a wave of sheer terror, the worst included an injured, possibly dead boy trapped in a car submerged in a water-filled ditch.

She dashed to the garage with Joe, the phone still glued

to her ear. She wasn't about to break the connection and leave Rose alone in the dark with her fears.

Except, she saw with a shock when Joe hit the garage opener and slammed his truck into gear, it wasn't dark. Squinting through the dazzling sunlight, Sue Ellen searched for the digital clock on the dash. Stunned, she realized a mere three hours had passed since Joe picked her up at work. It wasn't even eight-thirty yet, and the sky blazed with reds and golds of a brilliant summer evening.

As Joe wheeled around corners, following a route he'd obviously charted out in his head, Sue Ellen dragged the story out of Rose, detail by tragic detail.

She'd met Joan and the kids at Chuck E. Cheese at four-thirty, as agreed on.

Pus Face had sauntered in a few minutes later, saying his mom had included him in the invitation.

Rose had ignored him and concentrated on Bethie and the other kids.

He, evidently, had just been biding his time. When Joan and the kids drove off, he tried to muscle Rose into his rusty Camaro for a private party.

"Bastard," Sue Ellen muttered before she remembered the kid might be dead.

Hell! Dead or not, he was still a young thug.

"What happened then?" she asked Rose.

"Then I… Then I kneed him in the balls and ran to the Mustang."

Sue Ellen restrained her instinctive "good!" as Rose choked out the rest of the grim details.

"I guess I didn't hit him hard enough. All I did was make him mad. He crawled into his car and was right on my tail when I drove out of the parking lot. I… I didn't want him to follow me back to your condo. I didn't know if you were home and I was afraid he might, like, jump the curb and run over your mailbox or something. He's that stupid and mean, Sue Ellen."

"I know, Rose."

"I wanted to call you, warn you, but my purse had slipped under the seat. I couldn't reach it without letting go of the wheel and I didn't dare slow down or stop. He was right on my bumper."

The plea for understanding, for forgiveness, almost broke Sue Ellen's heart.

"I tried to lose him," Rose continued between shuddering sobs. "I thought maybe he might run out of gas or get lost or just give up. Then I ended up on this…this two-lane road, with nothing but woods on one side and the ditch on the other. That's when he rammed me."

"Bastard," Sue Ellen spit out again, with only a small dart of compunction this time.

"He's so *stupid*." Fury and fear reverberated through the desperate cry. "He didn't even *think* that slamming into the fender of a car going forty or fifty miles an hour might cause his junk heap to spin out of control."

"Is that what happened? His car spun out of control?"

"Yes." The rage left Rose's voice, leaving only the fear. "I hit a tree, and he went into the ditch. I couldn't get him out, Sue Ellen. I tried. I swear to God, I tried."

"I know you did! It was an accident. A horrible, tragic accident, but it wasn't your fault. When the police get there, you tell them exactly what happened. Do you hear me? Tell them the truth. Starting with the bruises Pus Face…"

What in hell was the kid's name? For the life of her, Sue Ellen couldn't remember.

"Starting with the bruises he put on your neck," she finished fiercely.

"I think I hear a siren now."

Panic colored every syllable.

"It's okay, Rose. It's okay. The police will help you. So will we. We're just…just…"

She flashed Joe a desperate question.

"Ten minutes out," he supplied, whipping onto a two-lane state road.

"Ten minutes," she told the girl. "We'll be there in ten minutes. Just tell the police officers exactly what happened."

"Okay. I'd better hang up now. They're here."

Sue Ellen snapped the phone shut, her stomach roiling. So many emotions clogged her throat she could barely grind out the guilt that now crushed her.

"I shouldn't have let Rose go to that pizza place alone. I shouldn't have let her take my car. She's a good driver. I made her test drive for a week before I turned over the keys, but I shouldn't have…"

"Watch the road," Joe cut in, ruthlessly stemming her tide of remorse. "We should hit another turnoff in about a half mile."

Her litany of guilt silenced, Sue Ellen squinted in the distance.

The turnoff was right where Joe had predicted. He cut right with a squeal of tires. The truck threw up a plume of white dust as it rattled down a narrow gravel road. Fifty yards down the road, a white sign with stark red lettering warned that they'd entered U.S. Government property.

Oh, God! No wonder Rose was lost. In her frantic attempt to evade her pursuer, she'd cut into the immense test range that covered more than five hundred square miles of the Florida Panhandle.

THE SCENE ON THE DESERTED stretch of unpaved road was right out of a nightmare.

The sun had slipped behind the tall pines crowding one side of the pavement. Deep shadows blanketed the road and made the flashing red-and-white strobes of the emergency vehicles appear all the more glaring and ominous. In addition to the police, a fire rescue unit had already responded. So, Sue Ellen saw, had a blue air force vehicle with Range Patrol lettering on its side panel.

She sprang out of Joe's truck as soon as he shoved it into Park. Her borrowed flip-flops whapping against gravel, she ran for the girl framed in the open rear door of a black-and-white squad car.

Rose saw her coming and leaped from the police car. Darting around a uniformed officer, she met Sue Ellen halfway and fell into her arms. Her weight and momentum almost dragged them both to the gravel, but Sue Ellen steadied herself and rocked Rose in her arms while shudder after shudder racked the girl's body.

While they remained locked together, Joe headed for the BDU-clad staff sergeant standing with two uniformed police officers. One of them, he noted grimly, dripped water from his hair and soaked uniform.

If Joe hadn't already identified the sergeant as Range Patrol, the holster strapped to the man's hip and M249 SAW racked in his vehicle would have clued him in. All military bases and units had stepped-up security in these dangerous times. The three major installations in the Pensacola-Fort Walton Beach area were no exception. Eglin, Hurlburt and Pensacola Naval Air Station all had vast permeable perimeters to defend.

Joe didn't recognize the sergeant, but he put an immediate name to the new arrival.

"Chief Goodwin! Did they call you to respond, too?"

Obviously the kid didn't know Joe had hung it up and was no longer on call to respond to military or civilian disaster.

"I'm not here in an official capacity." He jerked his head toward Rose. "I'm a friend of the girl's."

The dripping patrolman eyed Joe. "You the one who made the 911 call?"

"Yeah."

"Smart thinking, telling Dispatch to contact Hurlburt Ops. I don't know what kind of satellites you air force guys have up there, but Dispatch says they picked up the phone transmission in two minutes flat."

Joe didn't enlighten him. Spearing a glance at the vehicle nose down in the ditch at the side of the road, he saw it had sunk almost to its rear axle. Only a small portion of the roof showed.

Looking grim, Joe addressed the dripping police officer. "Did you get the kid out?"

"No."

When Joe spit out a curse favored by Special Ops, the cop gave a hasty explanation.

"We didn't get the kid out, because he wasn't in the car."

"What?"

"I went down three times to make sure. Looks like he kicked out a side window and wiggled through. We figure he either wandered off in a daze or took off running. We found some footprints, but they disappear into the pines."

"I called for a K-9 unit from Hurlburt," the staff sergeant put in. "They're on the way."

Joe's brows slashed down. "Something doesn't track here. Rose told us she tried to pull the kid out."

"She did. She was covered with mud and slime when we arrived. Problem is, the ditch water is murky as hell. She couldn't see the vehicle was empty. I could barely penetrate it with this baby."

Hefting a hand, he displayed a NexxtTech dual-powered 5-LED waterproof flashlight similar to those Special Tactics scuba teams took into the sea with them.

"I'm still not following this," Joe said, trying to fit the pieces together. "The driver of the submerged car escaped, but Rose didn't see him climb out of the ditch?"

In response, the officer aimed the flashlight and clicked it on. The powerful beam illuminated Sue Ellen's Mustang with its front end crumpled against a pine. The right rear fender showed a long paint scrape.

"Rose says she whacked her head against the windshield when she hit. She doesn't remember blacking out, but she must have. I'm betting the kid spotted her slumped over the wheel, panicked and fled the scene."

"Leaving her unconscious?"

Joe's second oath was considerably more vicious than the first. The sorry specimen Rose and Sue Ellen referred to as Pus Face had better pray like hell someone caught up with him before Joe did.

"Show me the footprints," he snarled.

From the corner of her eye, Sue Ellen spotted Joe stalking off with one of the uniformed officers.

She had a good idea where he was going. Rose had already supplied the incredible news that the police officers believed Brady Scott had survived his immersion. And that he'd apparently hightailed it into the woods.

Track him down, Joe. And when you find the little creep, I hope you beat him to a pulp.

Reining in her bloodthirsty thoughts, she walked Rose to the squad car and nudged her back down onto the seat. The interior lights illuminated the mud and pungent slime

Sue Ellen had sniffed in the girl's hair. It also illuminated the goose-egg-size lump on her forehead.

"Omigod! Did any of the rescue personnel take a look at your forehead?"

"One of the firemen did." Reaching up, Rose fingered the lump. "He thinks it's just a contusion, from when I hit the windshield, but says I should probably get X-rayed."

"You will! I'll talk to the police officers and see if…"

The rattle of tires careening over gravel cut her off. She turned to see a minivan come tearing down the road.

"Oh, no," Rose moaned. "It's Harvey and Joan. The police must have notified them."

Sue Ellen didn't see how the Scotts could have driven out here so quickly. Their place was a good twenty miles on the other side of Joe's. But there was no denying their presence when the minivan screeched to a halt and Joan erupted from the passenger seat. A round-shouldered man Sue Ellen assumed to be her husband slammed the driver-side door.

Both rushed toward the uniformed police officer. Halfway there, Joan spotted the two women and veered off. The light was now failing fast, but enough remained to illuminate the fury on the woman's face.

With a small animal sound, Rose scrambled off the car seat. Instinctively, Sue Ellen placed herself between the girl and her foster mother.

"You little bitch!"

Her fists balled, Joan stalked toward them.

"How could you do this? Didn't we take you in? Didn't we double up our own kids so you could have your own room? How could you do this?"

Sue Ellen held up a placating hand. "Hold on, Joan. I don't know what you think Rose did, but I can tell you…"

"I don't want you telling me anything! This is as much your fault as it is Rose's."

She had that right. Sue Ellen wasn't going to forgive herself anytime soon for letting Rose go for pizza without her.

"Brady told us how Rose goaded and goaded him," Joan raged. "How she showed off your fancy car and talked him into this stupid road race. He said she…"

"Wait a minute! Brady *called* you? When?"

"Right after Rose ran him off the road. He had my cell phone in his pocket. I make him take it whenever he's driving at night. He said he wasn't hurt, thank God, but Rose had banged her head and he was going for help. Harv and I bundled the kids over to a neighbor and jumped right in the van."

She whirled on Rose, her ire apparently undiminished by finding the girl relatively unhurt.

"You could have killed Brady. You're finished with us, you hear? Finished! I want you to pick up the rest of your things first thing tomorrow. If you don't, I'm throwing them out on the street."

Her foster daughter greeted the ultimatum with a stony silence. Sue Ellen wasn't as restrained.

"Hang on here, Joan. Brady lied to you. Rose didn't run him off the road. It was the other way around."

"Ha! Is that what she told you?"

"Yes."

"And you believe her? A runaway who stole a car and is a half step away from a juvenile detention center?"

"Damn straight, I believe her."

"Then you two deserve each other," Joan sneered. "Just make sure you keep her away from my kids. I don't want her around Bethie or Nick or Donny. Or Brady," she added, her lip curling.

That was too much for Rose.

"Don't worry! Your pimple-faced Peeping Tom is the last person on the planet I want to be around. You tell him to stay away from *me*. If he grabs me again, if he so much as *touches* me, I'm calling the cops!"

"Grabs you? Touches you?" Joan reeled back a step but recovered swiftly. "You're lying! Brady wouldn't hurt you or…or any of the kids."

Rose's mouth clamped shut, leaving Sue Ellen to disabuse the blind, doting parent.

"She's not lying, Joan. I saw the bruises on her neck when we first got to camp."

"I don't believe you. Either of you!"

Whirling, the woman rushed over to her husband. Sue Ellen only caught snatches of their agitated dialog, but the police officer's measured response had her sagging in relief. Although he wouldn't lay responsibility for the accident on either party at this point, he did hint that the physical evidence collected so far supported Rose's contention that she'd been sideswiped.

A much-subdued Joan clung to her husband's arm while he related what his son had told them. "Brady said Rose was hurt and he was going for help."

"In the woods?" Sue Ellen muttered to the girl beside her. "I don't *think* so. The little twerp is probably hiding under a log, waiting for Mommy and Daddy to arrive and bail him out of this mess."

Rose gave a hiccupping laugh that faded all too quickly. Her eyes were dark and unfathomable as she turned to Sue Ellen.

"No one's ever stood up for me before like you just did. I… Um… Thanks."

Feeling a thousand pounds lighter, Sue Ellen returned her awkward hug. "You're welcome."

Sue Ellen was half right, she discovered a short time later. Brady Boy *had* been hiding, but not under a log.

The sun had dropped out of the sky and the cicadas had set up a loud racket when three figures came out of the pines. A *very* scared-looking Brady with Joe and the police officer on either side.

When the kid spotted his parents, he burst into noisy sobs and galloped into their outstretched arms. Joe dusted his hands and joined the two women at the squad car.

"Dumb punk left a trail a mile wide. You could teach him a thing or two about covering his tracks, Rose."

Her snort conveyed a total lack of desire to teach Brady Scott anything.

"Where did you find him?" Sue Ellen asked.

"Crouched behind a rock. I sorta scared the kid, coming at him out of the dark the way I did." His mouth hitched in a slow, satisfied grin. "Hope his folks have some diapers in their minivan."

Torn between laughter and tears of relief that both teenagers had survived their ordeal relatively intact, Sue Ellen obtained the police officers' permission to take her charge to the ER for X rays.

She wedged into the narrow back seat of Joe's truck so Rose could stretch out in the front. Her frazzled nerves had calmed a little by the time she delivered Rose to the ER for the second time in as many months. They soothed completely after X rays confirmed the girl had sustained only a nasty contusion.

Both she and Rose were totally wiped when Joe pulled into the driveway of the condo. Sue Ellen waited for Rose to drag out of the front seat before wiggling her way out of the back. She had one oversize flip-flop on the ground when her cell phone pinged.

"This better not be the Scotts," she growled, digging in her purse. "I'm in no mood for belated concerns about what the X rays showed."

Feeling snarly all over again on Rose's behalf, she flipped up the lid. "Sue Ellen Carson."

"It's Doyle Andrews, Ms. Carson. I know it's late, but I thought you'd want to know I found Anna Maria Gutierrez."

Her second major shock of the evening left Sue Ellen spaghetti-kneed. Stunned, she slumped against the truck door.

"Are you serious?"

"Yes, ma'am. She's in a nursing home south of Tampa. After her daughter OD'd and it got around she didn't have any living relatives who cared what happened to her, some shyster lawyer got himself appointed her guardian. From what I've been able to piece together, he sold her house out from under her and put her in the nursing home. They mixed up her social security with another patient's, which is why it took me so long to find her."

He paused, and Sue Ellen stared slack-jawed at Rose and Joe. Before she could gather her wits enough to explain her stupefaction, Andrews delivered the night's third major blow.

"She's in pretty bad shape, Ms. Carson. If you want to reunite her with her granddaughter, you'd better get Rose down here pretty quick."

Her heart sinking like a stone, Sue Ellen got the name and location of the nursing home from Andrews and hung up.

"Back in the truck, you two. We're driving to Tampa. I'll explain why on the way."

Three jam-packed months later, a hot August sun blazed down on Sue Ellen as she marshaled her troops.

The Blues were gathered to unload the spiffy silver Audi TT Coup that had replaced her Mustang. It was filled with props for their presentation, but Sue Ellen's primary concern was the rubber plant protruding from the Audi's passenger-side window.

"Careful with that, Ev. Ralph is too old and creaky to be manhandled."

The beefy football player decked out in a Florida Gator's athletic shirt rolled his eyes. "You heard the lady, Jackson. Take hold of the stalk while I lift out the rest of...uh..."

"Ralph," Sue Ellen supplied, stroking a glossy leaf. Then she directed the remaining Blues to the display boards bubble-wrapped in the Audi's trunk.

The two Pauls hefted one, Roger and Dylan the other. Brenda and her mom extracted the peripheral pieces. Sue

Ellen tucked a paper-wrapped bundle under her arm and beeped the trunk closed.

The Blues were about to give their fifteenth presentation of the Northwest Florida Cultural Heritage Interactive Display. They'd sweated blood over the multidimensional, computer-driven video program, working out bugs in each of their previous presentations. In the process, they'd all increased their knowledge of Florida's rich heritage by exponential degrees. Now they'd share that knowledge with the patrons of the Gulf Breeze Community Center.

First, however, Sue Ellen needed to deliver Ralph to one of the pink-and-white cottages clustered near the Center The mayor of Gulf Breeze had designated the cottages as low-income housing.

It was a wrench to part with her faithful companion. He'd seen her through some grim times.

"Can you guys handle setup?" she asked her fellow Blues.

"We got it," Paul Jr. assured her. "You do what you need to do."

"Okay. Ev, Jackson, it's the third unit on the right."

As she led them toward the two-bedroom cottage, Sue Ellen once again marveled at the miracle her friend had accomplished in such a short space of time. Andi, bless her determined military soul, had twisted arms at HUD to push through approval of the low-income designation. Sue Ellen had done her part by calling every pal in Washington to grease the skids. Now financially constrained residents could afford to live in neat, well-maintained homes.

One of those residents yanked open the door as Sue Ellen trooped up the walk with Ev, Jackson and Ralph. Rose had bloomed in the three months since she'd swept into the nursing home and announced she was there to see her grandmother.

Her eyes dancing, Rose held the door open. "I can't believe you're really parting with Ralph."

"He needs love and attention."

"And we need the space."

That came from Joe, who appeared from the interior of the cottage. He'd come over earlier to set up the book-shelves he'd salvaged from his house before putting it on the market.

He'd plowed the hefty profit right into STEP, almost matching the federal funds DOL had supplied. In two months, he'd conducted two additional Phase One camps while personally monitoring the progress of every previous participant.

Between camps, he'd moved into Sue Ellen's condo.

That was on the market now, too. As Joe said, they needed more space. They'd probably get around to marriage, too. One of these days. His unrepentant, unapologetic you're-my-woman-now attitude was gradually wearing down her resistance.

"How's your grandmother today?"

"This is a good day," Rose said on a rush of emotion. "We talked about my mom while Joe was setting up the shelves. She told me things I never knew. Good things."

Sue Ellen had harbored serious doubts about Rose's insistence that she be allowed to live with her grandmother. So had her caseworker.

Rose had proved them both wrong. She was used to taking care of herself, she'd argued, *and* a houseful of kids. She could take care of a grandmother whose frighteningly debilitated condition stemmed from neglect and malnourishment, according to the geriatric specialist they'd taken Anna Maria to.

She was still heart-stoppingly frail, but three months of loving care had brought color back into her papery cheeks and joyous wonder to her eyes when they rested on her granddaughter. It was there now as Rose crouched beside her chair.

"Look what Sue Ellen brought us, Grandma. His name is Ralph."

"The plant has a name?"

"He's an old friend," Sue Ellen explained as the McPhee

brothers stood patiently with their burden. "Where would you like him?"

Anna Maria didn't hesitate. She and Rose had already made the cottage into a home. Their home.

"Over by the window, so he gets the morning sunlight."

Sue Ellen experienced another pang when Ev and Jackson set Ralph in the designated spot, but it lasted only until Joe looped an arm around her waist.

"He looks good there."

"Ha! Don't try to butter me up. I know you just want his space for your filing cabinets."

Joe didn't bother to deny the accusation. Most of his important papers and personal belongings were in boxes stacked in the alcove office they now shared. His clothes were split between the guest room closet and the space Sue Ellen had carved out of the master bedroom walk-in. His furniture had gone in a rented storage unit until they decided what to do with it.

In the space of a few months, she thought ruefully, a sullen teen and a man with a vision had turned her neat, well-ordered world upside down.

Thank God!

Drawing strength and joy from Joe's solid presence, she leaned into his side…and immediately jumped away. A sharp prick reminded her of the paper-wrapped object under her arm.

"I almost forgot. We don't want Ralph to lack for friends of the green variety. If you plant this right outside the window, you and your grandmother could enjoy it, too."

Rose took the package she offered with a questioning look.

"Go ahead," Sue Ellen urged, "unwrap it. Just watch out for the thorns."

Paper gave way to burlap, burlap to a bundled stalk of twigs. Rose stared at the bare stalks for long moments. When she finally spoke, her voice was thick with emotion.

"You remembered?"

"I remembered." Sue Ellen felt her throat close. "It's a hybrid tea rose. I had it shipped in from Tyler, Texas. The name of the variety is on the tag."

Rose turned over the plastic tag and read the name.

"Grandmother's Garden."

When both women burst into tears, Anna Maria clucked in distress, the McPhee brothers looked profoundly uncomfortable, and Joe reached in his back pocket. Ever the instructor, he passed Sue Ellen a handkerchief and grinned at Ev and Jackson.

"Always go in prepared for the worst, guys."

Silhouette® Desire

You can lead a horse to water...

When Alyssa Barkley and Clint Westmoreland
found out that their "fake" marriage was never
rendered void, they are forced to live together
for thirty days. However, Clint loves the single
life and has no intention of being tamed, but
when Alyssa moves in, the sizzling attraction
between them is ignited and neither wants the
thirty days to end.

Look for

TAMING CLINT WESTMORELAND

by

BRENDA JACKSON

Available February wherever you buy books

Silhouette®

Romantic
SUSPENSE

**Sparked by Danger,
Fueled by Passion.**

When Tech Sergeant Jacob "Mako" Stone opens
his door to a mysterious woman without a past,
he knows his time off is over. As threats to Dee's
life bring her and Jacob together, she must set
aside her pride and accept the help of the military
hero with too many secrets of his own.

Out of Uniform
by Catherine Mann

Available February wherever you buy books.

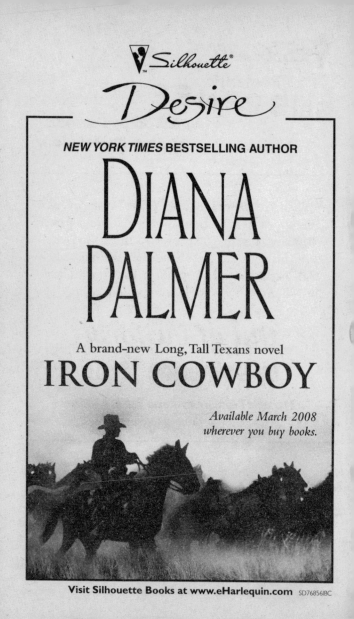

Silhouette® Desire

NEW YORK TIMES BESTSELLING AUTHOR

DIANA PALMER

A brand-new Long, Tall Texans novel

IRON COWBOY

Available March 2008
wherever you buy books.